King of the Wild

BY THE SAME AUTHOR

ICE TREK

For Andrew

I see the grass shake in the sun for leagues on either hand,
I see a river loop and run about a treeless land–
An empty plain, a steely pond, a distance diamond clear,
And low blue naked hills beyond. And what is that to fear?

The Prairie
Rudyard Kipling

1

Caribou

They came in a rolling swirling tide of living flesh, cresting the summit of the ridge and flowing on down to where the tundra stretched north to the frozen sea. They came swiftly, a grunting, lowing, clicking horde, their hooves cutting the tender skin of the earth, wearing away the moss and lichen and thin peaty soil until the barren rock lay naked under the sky. Their numbers were so vast, their ranks so tightly packed, that the heat of their bodies formed a cloud, a mist of vapour that drifted above them and froze on the bitter Arctic air.

Behind them lay a journey, a long and arduous trek over mountain and plain, across river and lake and sand bar, through thickets of willow and spruce and alder, over vast distances untrodden by man, and as they journeyed north the woods grew thinner, the trees shorter, until, stunted to ground level by the cold and crippling winds, they ceased to grow altogether.

They had passed the winter sheltering in small bands among the dense forests that bordered a great river to the south, snatching a frugal living from the twigs of bushes that showed above the snow. Then, as the days began to lengthen with the coming of the spring, they had grown increasingly restless with the urge to travel north. Small groups began to gather, twos and threes forming bands of a dozen or more, the bands uniting in herds, the herds melding and mingling, until, to the thunder of countless hooves, the spring migration of the caribou had begun.

Throughout the length and breadth of Arctic America other widely scattered herds were on the move, small

1

bands sometimes coalescing to form a mighty horde such as this. Some made even longer journeys, travelling north until they reached the shores of the Beaufort Sea. Some did not journey so far, contenting themselves by moving out of the sheltered valleys and up into the windswept hills. Either way, by doing so they left behind the worst heat of the summer, and escaped many of the predators, wolf and lynx and bear, which together with the biting flies threatened the survival of their calves. Furthermore, by vacating their winter feeding grounds, they gave the land time to make new growth and provide fresh browse on their return.

The cows led, those heavy with calf, for their need was most urgent. Far behind came the stragglers, the old barren cows, the yearlings and the larger bulls. Many died on the way, taken by lynx or wolf or bear, or swept away at river crossings, or drowned when melting ice broke under their weight. Some were simply too old, too tired and worn to continue further, so they lay down and died, and the ravens picked their bones. Only the young, the strong, survived, yet still, as the miles passed beneath their hooves and day followed day their numbers seemed beyond counting, their columns as endless as the hills that lay beyond.

Then, suddenly, it was over. The throng slowed, milled irresolute for a time, and then, like smoke stirred by an idle wind, individual cows broke from the herd and trotted purposefully away, as if suddenly desperate to find solitude and concealment, diminishing in size as they distanced themselves from their companions, dwindling to mere dots on the distant horizon, disappearing among the hills and hummocks of the undulating terrain. So vast was the landscape, so immeasurable the miles that stretched on all sides, that soon it seemed no life existed at all in that bleak inhospitable land.

2

Yet life was there, and before the new moon waxed to full that complement of life would double, as the scattered cows gave birth to their calves. Those which had led the migration would give birth first, thus ensuring that their offspring would get the very best start in life, and the maximum period of growth during the short Arctic summer. Furthermore, those cows which had given birth before knew from experience where, in that seemingly featureless land, the safest, the most sheltered nooks and crannies lay.

One such individual hastened now to the site where, in previous years, she had given birth, a low outcrop of weather-worn rock and scree, that broke the pitiless winds and gave shelter to a dense mat of dwarf willow, which in turn would shield the body of her calf. Her time was not yet due, but in the interval she would guard her chosen spot with the fierce pride of possession, driving away latecomer cows with a vigour that brooked no defiance.

She was travel-worn and weary, her coat harsh and staring, faded with the passage of time. Her swollen belly served only to accentuate her extreme emaciation, for the winter had been cold and hard, and throughout the long, arduous journey north there had been little time to browse.

Now she was able to rest, and feed on the lichens and ground-hugging plants that carpeted the tundra. Around her other cows awaited their confinement, uniformly scattered across the land. Though spring was almost over the weather remained chill, with overcast skies, and low clouds which brought showers of hail and stinging snow, borne on the relentless wind. The ground here was elevated and dry, sloping almost imperceptibly to an endless tussocky quagmire, a slobbery waterlogged land overlaying the permafrost, where innumerable lakes gleamed leaden in the grey diffused light.

The cow was impervious to the cold. Her dense pelage was composed of hollow guard hairs, overlaying a thick

3

mantle of dense curly underfur. Even the skin of her muzzle was covered in fine hair, and enlarged nasal cavities warmed the frozen air she breathed, protecting her lungs from harm. Her great hooves, which would carry her in safety over deep snow or marshy ground, insulated her from the frost. The days passed in waiting and in comfort, the only sounds the thin keening of the wind, the call of a loon, the distant howl of a wolf, and the harsh note of the ravens, ever winging their way across the empty canopy of the sky.

The birth, when it came, was over quickly. One moment the mother was grazing quietly in the thin light of dawn. Suddenly she stopped, head and neck outstretched, and gave a loud coughing bellow of protest and pain. Then she lay down, and the matted leaves of the willow hid her from view. Minutes later she was standing again, trembling a little from exertion and shock, and there at her feet lay a fine bull calf, soaking wet and steaming in the cold morning air. He was her third calf, and his name was Anak.

Roughly she groomed him, licking the moisture from his hair until it glowed a soft reddish brown, and soon, under the stimulus of her tongue he was able to rise shakily to his feet and wag his short tail. In a very little while he was feeding, sucking greedily at her flank and filling his small frame with rich yellow milk.

He gained strength by the minute, so that after an hour he was able to trot without stumbling, following his mother as she grazed, and within two days he was so fleet of foot he could easily outdistance a man. For the moment though he was content to stay close by his mother's side, to seek out the milk she so readily gave, and to sleep curled up in the shelter of the rocks.

He was a big calf, and by the end of a fortnight he had doubled his birth weight of fourteen pounds. Across the

tundra, as far as the eye could see, all the other cows had given birth to their calves.

From a far-off hill a young Eskimo watched the caribou herd, but though his saliva ran, and his stomach knotted and cramped at the sight of so much meat, he knew he had found them too late. Distance diminished the size of the deer, so that they resembled mouse-grey maggots slowly crawling across the mouldering hide of some long-dead beast. Though his bow and spear lay near to his hand he was now too weak even to crawl across the stretch of tundra that lay between him and the herd.

His name was Ootek, and he had been born and raised in a village far away on the edge of the sea. Life had been good then. In the spring had come the white whales, providing a mountain of flesh for all. Then there had been the seals, and great flocks of migrating birds and their eggs. There had been fish and hares and berries from the hill, and each summer the grey deer had arrived to drop their calves, a rich harvest of meat and hides. Always by the time of the long winter night the lodges of the people had been crammed with stocks of good things to eat.

Then, the previous spring, three boats had followed the whales as they swam north along the coast. They were big boats, far bigger than any Ootek had ever seen before, blown on sails by the wind, and crewed by white, bearded strangers. These men hunted the whales, and melted down the blubber in great steaming cauldrons they set up along the shore.

They hunted seal and walrus too, and all that summer the men and women of the village helped them in their work, until the sea was stained red, and piles of bones and mounds of decaying meat littered the high tide mark. In return for their help the white men gave them many presents, beads and mirrors for the women, axes and sharp knives for the men, and so eager were the people to possess these treasures that they worked even harder

5

than before. They no longer hunted merely for food but for furs to trade, and deer for the white men, who did not like meat that tasted of the sea. Some, the older and wiser, worried over the lack of provision for the hard times to come, but the others just laughed at their fears. Did not the white strangers provide more meat than the people could eat? Indeed the slaughter was so great that much meat was wasted. There would be plenty of time to hunt for themselves before the winter came. Meanwhile there were richer prizes to be won.

The short summer passed swiftly. The sun sank ever lower in the sky, the nights grew longer, and ice began to form on the edges of the sea. Then, one morning, the people woke to find the white men had gone. Where the ships had laid at anchor in the bay there was nothing but sea and sky, and the people did not understand. They thought they must have offended or angered their guests for them to depart so suddenly. For a long time they watched and waited for the ships to return, but day followed day without any sign of a sail on the horizon, and they realized at last that they waited in vain.

That year the onset of winter was stormy, and for days and nights on end the wind blew from the sea, sending great waves crashing against the shore, and hurling sheets of frozen, stinging spray across the land. Until the wind died no ice could form on the turbulent waters, and the people stayed in their lodges, huddled together for warmth, unable to hunt for food. A few families, more prudent than the rest, had laid in some supplies against this time, but their stores did not last long when shared among so many.

When at last the wind died, and the surface of the sea froze hard enough to bear a man's weight, the hunters who ventured out on the ice all returned with the same tale. There were no seals. Too many had been killed the previous summer, and those that had survived were too few and scattered to be found.

That winter the people knew real hunger for the first time. They were reduced, first to eating their dogs, then strips of hide, and shreds of putrefied meat from the carcases that still littered the beach. They had no fuel to burn, for the whalers had gleaned every scrap of the driftwood that was normally to be found along the shore, using it to heat their cauldrons.

Soon people began to fall sick. They grew weak, and started to cough, and after a while they spat up blood and died. It was then that Ootek's father made up his mind. 'There is nothing here for us except slow death,' he announced. 'We will go inland, and seek out the great deer herds that live in the distant hills.'

So early one morning, when a waning moon bathed the land in glittering light, Ootek, his father and mother and young sister set off across the rolling tundra, carrying with them what few possessions they could manage. At first they fared better. They shot hares and ptarmigan with their bows, and once they found the frozen carcase of a caribou, half-eaten by the wolves. Yet despite the food, Ootek's mother grew weaker, and soon she too began to cough. One morning they woke to find her frozen corpse huddled among her sleeping robes. Next Ootek's sister died.

Now Ootek and his father travelled on alone. Spring came and the days grew rapidly longer, but the weather seemed to get worse, with an icy wind whipping up frozen snow and blinding them until they were forced to dig a shelter in the snow and lie there for days on end. When the wind abated they set off once more, but they were weaker now, and still there was no sign of the deer herds they had come so far to find. They ate berries, frozen on the bushes swept clear of snow, leaves and moss and even small twigs. Occasionally they killed a hare, and once a fox.

7

One night, before they settled to sleep, Ootek's father held out a short length of rawhide thong. 'Tie my hands,' he ordered.

Ootek took the cord, wondering at this strange request. 'Why?' he queried.

His father shrugged. 'I have it in mind to kill you while you sleep, and eat your flesh. I do not want to do this, but I cannot promise that I will not.'

Ootek fingered the cord for a moment. 'What if I kill you?' he asked.

'I would not blame you,' his father replied.

So each night thereafter Ootek solemnly tied his father's wrists, and often he thought of killing him and feeding on his flesh. Yet the more he considered it, the more repellent the idea became. Now he had no more need of the cord, and his father no need of his flesh. Still Ootek found himself unable to take advantage of the fact. He lay there in the shelter of the rocks, and watched the deer, and wondered how long before he too would die.

A shadow flickered across the face of the sun, and Ootek awakened from his reverie. His eyes, sunk deep in their sockets, narrowed in interest as a raven pitched on the ground close to his father's corpse. Slowly, never taking his eyes from the bird, Ootek reached down and groped around until his questing fingers closed over his bow. The raven had not seen him. Intent on its feast, it hopped closer, as Ootek notched an arrow to the bowstring.

He scarcely had the strength to bend the bow. As he drew it back the muscles in his arm began to tremble with weakness. The arrow flew straight, but it lacked power, and the raven hopped nonchalantly aside as the arrow flew past, to break itself among the stones. Almost sobbing with despair Ootek rested awhile, flexing his fingers and the muscles of his arm.

Emboldened, the raven came again, nearer now. Ootek took a deep breath, and summoning every ounce of his will, drew back the bow and fired. Almost, the raven managed to dodge out of the way again, but its timing was just a fraction slow. The arrow caught it in one wing, tumbling it over in flight, so that it fell in a crumpled heap among the stones. In an instant Ootek flung himself upon it, and in one swift movement tore its head off. His lips closed around its neck as the blood spurted from its still quivering corpse.

The flesh was rancid and stringy, but he had eaten worse, and he managed to finish it all, bones and innards and even some of the feathers. When it was all gone he slept for a while, and when he woke he felt stronger. He lingered for a while, still drowsy, breathing a heartfelt prayer of thanks to his father, who had unwittingly provided a lifesaving meal. He wanted to give the body a proper burial, but the ground was frozen hard and he lacked the strength even to cover it with stones. With a sigh of regret he turned away, resolving to return if he should survive.

He picked up his bow and spear and set out across the tundra towards the deer, but after only a few yards he realized he was much weaker than he had thought. His feet faltered and tripped. Several times he stumbled and fell sprawling in the snow. Each time he lay there, sobbing with frustration, until his strength returned and he was able to rise and stagger a few more feet.

Throughout most of the day he persisted, crawling, walking, sometimes resting for long periods, slowly drawing nearer to the grazing herd. Each time he fell he lay, thinking he would never be able to rise again. Yet he knew that to lie still was to die. He had to reach the herd. Somehow he had to get near them without panicking them into flight, to find some place of concealment where he could lie in wait, and then hope that one would stray within bow shot. Beyond that he did not dare think.

9

Slowly he drew nearer, until at last he could hear the grunting of the caribou cows, and the click of their hooves as they moved. Now the curve of the hill hid them from view. What slight wind there was blew on his face, and he welcomed this, for there was little chance of the deer catching his scent. He crawled all the time now, keeping his head down, his face almost brushing the frozen moss and the short wiry grasses of the tundra.

A little to one side he spied a clump of grey weather-worn boulders, cresting the ridge of the hill, and he made his way towards these, hoping for some vantage point from which to view the deer. He rested a while in their shelter, summoning all his reserves of strength before raising his head and peering out over the ridge. It was better than he had hoped. A cow grazed near, her calf loitering at her heel. They were both within bow shot, if only he could find the strength to bend the bow.

For a long while he watched them, wondering whether to take the cow or the calf. The cow was the easier target, but he was not sure if he could send the arrow with sufficient force to drive it through her hide. The calf was young, no more than a fortnight old, but it was a big one, and its meat would sustain him for several days. He debated whether or not to try and narrow the gap. He decided not. The cow had ceased grazing and was standing, head alert, listening, though he was sure he had made no sound. He notched an arrow to his bow and took careful aim at the calf.

At that precise moment the cow gave a short, warning bark. Both she and the calf turned and ran. Ootek stared in dismay. Looking out over the hill he saw that the whole herd was running, fleeing from some unseen threat, an enemy who had just snatched away his last chance of life. Then, as he stood there, tears of frustration and rage slowly trickling down his cheeks, he heard a murmur of sound. It was vaguely familiar, but it was so long since

10

he had heard it last that it was some time before he recognized it for what it was, the mingling of laughter and human voices.

People were coming, and without caring whether they were friend or foe he stood up and half stumbled, half ran towards the sound. He had a fleeting impression of astonished faces, of a group of small brown people dressed in ragged furs and skins, and an excited babbling in a tongue that he did not understand. Then the whole world turned grey, the ground rose to meet him, and he pitched headlong in their midst.

2

The Reindeer Herder

Carver Calthorpe shook his hand free of his frozen mitt, broke the film of ice that encased his beard and moustache, and thrust a short black pipe in the hole thus provided. The pipe was ready packed, and needed only the application of a match to make it draw sweetly. Carver was a man who believed in planning ahead, a short wiry weasel of a man with piercing blue eyes, whose sandy beard was at odds with the matted greying locks beneath his parka hood. Any fool could be uncomfortable in the wilderness, he reasoned, any raw *cheechako*, any green tenderfoot could survive, for a while at least, before he made his last fatal mistake. Mother Nature, he was wont to proclaim, was a hard bitch to serve, but a fair one. Get it right, and you could have a good time. Get it wrong, and she'd kill you.

Getting it right meant planning ahead, and to be able to plan ahead meant leading an ordered existence. So, once his pipe was alight, he set about unharnessing his dogs and staking them out in the snow, far enough apart so that they would not fight, before throwing each of them a lump of frozen fish. Only then did he turn his attention to making camp.

Given a map, it was unlikely that he could have shown you exactly where he was, but he was on familiar territory right now. He knew every creek and slough and gravel bar, every muskeg swamp and stand of willow, every rock and hill and bend in the river. He knew the weather too. An hour earlier he had detected a slight change in the wind, a softening that heralded snow. So, although daylight had yet some hours to run, he had turned aside from the trail and headed towards a low stand of spruce, set in the lee of a hill which would shelter him from the blizzard he was sure was going to blow.

He worked methodically, seemingly without haste, yet in a very short while he had cleared a platform in the snow, set up a wall of snow blocks, and stretched a tarpaulin over the whole. He cut soft spruce boughs for a bed, and covered them with a moose hide. Then he foraged around until he found a dead poplar, with which he built a base, and on this he laid his fire.

He gathered the beans he had boiled the night before, and then spread upon the snow to freeze. He had bacon, and pig fat which he melted in his frying pan before putting the bacon on to fry. When the bacon was cooked he threw in the beans, and in less than ten minutes he was eating his meal. Meantime he had packed his dixie with snow, and set it in the embers of the fire to boil. He had tea and sugar and salt and flour, and ammunition and matches to spare, and he could survive for months if need be.

Before he brewed his tea he set about gathering a supply of fuel for the night, spruce for a quick blaze, slow-burning poplar to keep the embers glowing red, stacking the logs close at hand, so he could make up the fire without crawling from his bed. He had just fetched the last armful when the snow came, small stinging flakes blowing horizontally across the land, eddying in gusts around the trees and hissing as they struck the flames of the fire. Then larger flakes began to fall, dark against the sky, grey goose feathers swirling in the wind. He sat snug in the confines of his *killigun*, sipping his tea, secure against the weather but uneasy in his mind.

He was a fur trapper, but he had not been one all his life. Once he had owned a small farm, a quarter section he had inherited from his father. Here, twenty years ago, he had brought his bride, a young girl fresh from city life. At first they had been happy together, but that year and the next had been drought years, and as the corn withered on the stalks so his wife's love for him shrivelled and died. One spring morning, when he was out ploughing the rich black soil of the prairie with his team of mules, she had taken their small store of savings, hitched the buggy to the mare and driven off to the nearest town.

He never saw her again. He learned later that she had caught a train back east, but no one knew where. For a while he lingered on at the farm, but he had lost all interest in his work, and at night the loneliness of the deserted house and the ticking of the clock on the wall drove him half out of his mind. One night he took his gun and blew the clock off the wall, and next morning he sold the mules, saddled up the mare and rode away from the farm, leaving the corn crop to the crows.

As a boy he had snared muskrats round the farm, and later an old Indian had taught him how to trap beaver, otter, mink and fox, a harvest which provided him with pocket money and enabled him to buy his first gun. Now, in his wanderings, he rediscovered his old skills, living off the land, always earning enough to grubstake himself for another year, but never making enough to settle down.

So far he had not wanted to. The restlessness that had filled him after the departure of his wife had never quite left him. He had never remarried, unless you counted the occasional interlude spent with a companionable squaw. Indeed, he saw little of his fellow white men, preferring to live with the Indians, and, some said, even beginning to think like one.

All the time there was the lure of far-off lands, a longing to see round the next bend of the stream, to gaze on the view that lay hidden beyond the distant hills. Always at the back of his mind was the hope that one day he would discover some unexplored valley, an Eldorado rich in furs, a mine of soft gold that would keep him in luxury for the rest of his life. Meantime he kept looking.

Each year it was the same. If prices were high, pelts were scarce. If the trapping season had been good, prices were low. This year prices seemed set to go sky high, for good pelts had never been harder to obtain. There were no mink, no otter, and no wolf. Lynx were few and far between, and even foxes were hard to find.

He knew the cause. Ever since the Dane, Vitus Bering, had reported a great land to the east of the straits that now bore his name, white men had come to plunder that land of its natural wealth, robbing and enslaving the natives in the process. Even after secretary of state William Seward had bought the land from the Russians in 1867 men of all nations had continued the pillage, venturing further and further north. First it had been the whalers, scouring the frozen seas in search of whale oil and baleen. Then came traders, sailing along the coast and calling at each village along the way, trading with the natives for fine furs. In return they offered rifles and shotguns, powder and lead, knives of steel and cooking pots of iron, fish hooks, harpoon heads, axes, mirrors, tobacco and beads. Worse, they brought rum, and once the natives got a taste for it, the traders supplied molasses and taught them how to distil their own liquor.

Once addicted, Eskimo and Indian alike gave up all thought of hunting for food, turning to the trapline instead, and if they did hunt for caribou or seal, it was only to trade the meat for more drink. Since the traders were many, there was always a demand for meat, and near the coast the caribou herds were decimated, the whole land hunted out. Then the traders sailed away, and the natives were left to starve.

Those that did survive, those who could still find enough meat to keep themselves alive, found that the traders had left them a parting gift. Sometimes it was whooping cough, sometimes tuberculosis, smallpox, measles or influenza. Often it was syphilis or gonorrhoea, for the native women

15

soon discovered that they had goods other than furs to trade for rum.

More than thirty years had passed since America had purchased Alaska from the Russians. In the closing years of the nineteenth century gold had been discovered, first on the Yukon, near the Canadian border, and then on the beaches of Nome, far to the west. In response to its lure, thousands of men had poured into the country, hungry, desperate men ill-equipped to cope with the savagery of the climate or the vastness of the land. Many died, but many more came to take their place, though few got rich.

For all these reasons Carver stayed well away from the coast, but even this far inland the blight was beginning to make itself felt in this winter of 1902. Unless things improved dramatically he would be forced to make a move, but where he was not as yet sure. For the moment he was just prospecting, travelling over the frozen land in search of some forgotten corner of the wilderness where fur bearers were still plentiful. He finished the last of his tea and knocked out the embers of his pipe before recharging it again and putting it away. Darkness was falling. It was time to dust the snow off his hot-water bottle.

This was Handsome, his lead dog. Five years previously, Carver had acquired a German Shepherd bitch, and when she came in season Carver had tied her to a tree outside his cabin. That night a he-wolf came calling, and stayed with the bitch throughout the following day. During that time they mated twice, and on the third occasion Carver crept up behind the couple and killed the wolf with a club. He had served his purpose, Carver reasoned, and his pelt was prime.

The result of this alliance was Handsome, an animal of such evil disposition that he was known and feared throughout the length and breadth of North–West Alaska. Carver had lost count of the number of other dogs he had killed. He attacked natives on sight, and had bitten three

16

white men. Once a year, when the wolves were breeding, Handsome would bite through his trace and disappear for days at a time. He would return torn and bleeding from countless bites, but always with such an air of satisfaction that Carver did not have the heart to chastise him. For his part Handsome never once bit Carver.

From early puppyhood Handsome had shared Carver's bed whenever they were on the trail. As well as keeping Carver warm, Handsome served as bodyguard, warning his master of the approach of thieving Indian or marauding bear. He stank abominably, but as Carver said, 'Damn dog smells like a badly kept drain, but then so do I, so I reckon we deserve each other.'

By morning the blizzard had blown itself out. Not a breath of wind stirred, and a pale sun shone through the ice-laden air. Soft powdery snow lay in deep drifts, and Carver had to jog in front of his team, breaking the trail with his snowshoes. The way ahead lay over low hills, devoid of any vegetation, interspersed with wide valleys cloaked with dense thickets of willow and scrub poplar. Though it was extra weight to carry, Carver kept his rifle slung over his shoulder. It was getting late for bear, but the thickets made excellent cover for moose, and a bull moose could be one of the most dangerous creatures he was likely to meet.

He came out of the trees, and the spectacle that confronted him was so astounding that he could only stand and gape, stopping so suddenly that the dogs behind him almost ran him down. Ahead lay a small plain, where a herd of some sixty caribou stood scraping at the ground, shovelling away the snow to get at the lichen buried underneath. It was not the sight of the meat that had arrested him however, but another drama being enacted close to. At the edge of the willows lay a wide creek, its frozen surface covered in snow, save for one spot, a little way downstream, where a gaping black hole had appeared

17

in the ice. Beside the hole, straining on a rawhide rope, stood a gaunt, long-legged scarecrow of a man clad in tattered skins. As Carver watched, the man slid slowly, inexorably, ever nearer the hole.

Without pausing to consider, Carver leaped upon the sledge, mushed his dogs into a fast run and careered down the slope on to the creek, hoping his speed would carry him across to the other side before the ice gave way. As he did so he heard a crack and a splintering of ice, together with a long despairing cry, and he glanced across just in time to see the stranger, still clinging to the rope, plunge head first into the creek.

Carver flung his sledge over on one side, bringing his dogs to an abrupt halt, and threw himself flat on the ice, arms and legs spread wide apart, easing himself forward to the edge of the hole, where icy green water bubbled and swirled. A head appeared briefly, waving tendrils of long black hair, and Carver grabbed hold.

The rest was easy. The water at the edge of the ice was only waist deep, and once the stranger found a footing he was able, in spite of the strong current, to help himself out. For a while neither man spoke. Each knew the dangers of death by frostbite after such an immersion, and for a while both men were fully occupied. While the stranger stripped off his furs, Carver untied his moose robe from the sledge and flung it to him. Then he busied himself lighting a fire.

Fortunately the banks of the creek were littered with driftwood, swept down by the floods of the previous spring and half-buried in the snow. Carver kindled a good blaze and put a brew of tea on to boil. Then he lit his pipe and waited for the stranger to stop shaking. All the while he was studying him, noting the dark Mongolian eyes set above high cheekbones, the lack of hair on the face and chin, the complexion, too dark for a white man; yet there was something about him that was not quite right. A half-breed, Carver guessed, they were not uncommon nowadays.

18

When the tea was ready he poured out a mug and passed it across. 'You Eskimo, or Siwash, or what?' he queried.

The stranger accepted the tea and sipped it gratefully. 'Neither, sir,' he replied, 'though you may be pardoned for thinking so. In fact I am a Siberian, a Chukchi from across the sea. My name is Abner, and may I say how grateful I am for your timely assistance in rescuing me from my plight.'

Carver retrieved his pipe from where it had fallen in his lap. For a moment he was uncertain whether or not he was being made a victim of some ingenious leg pull, though this hardly seemed the time or the place. He decided he was not. The man was being truly sincere. There could only be one explanation.

'You a preacher then?'

Abner smiled and shook his head. 'No, but I was taught what little English I know by a Presbyterian minister, a devout but wholly misguided man. It was he who gave me my name, since he was unable to pronounce my real one.'

Carver digested this in silence for a while. Opposite him Abner sat drinking his tea, wrapped in the moose-hide robe. He seemed suddenly to have slumped into an attitude of utter dejection, his face lifeless, his thoughts far away. In the distance the caribou herd still grazed over the plain, and Carver was just thinking that it would be a good time to put his rifle to use when Abner gave a shrill whistle.

Immediately two small dogs appeared from where they had lain hidden in the snow, and racing off, they circled the herd of deer and began driving them back towards the two men. Then, at a further command, the dogs ran to join Abner, nestling at his feet as he sat by the fire.

Suddenly Carver understood. 'You're a reindeer herder,' he exclaimed.

Abner nodded. 'Always, my people have been reindeer herders. One day, some years ago, two men came to my village wanting to buy deer. One was a white man, a stout,

19

fussy little preacher. Not the one who taught me English, you understand, but another, more important. The other was a black man, a big man who was captain of a ship. They told us that the people here were starving, that the wild deer had all gone, and that they wanted to introduce reindeer in order to provide meat.

'At first my people did not want to sell their herds. After all, money was no use to them, but by and by the strangers produced goods, fine knives and axes of steel, and many other things my people coveted. So at last they relented, and sold some of their deer. Then the white men said they wanted herdsmen, young men who were prepared to look after the deer when they were shipped across the sea, but no one would go. Everyone had families, friends, people they did not want to leave. All, that is, except me. Both my parents were dead, and I had no wife or children to care for, no deer of my own to tend. So I came, to seek my fortune in this new world.'

Carver nodded; he had heard about the scheme to introduce reindeer to Alaska. From the start he had felt that the project was doomed to failure, and indeed he had heard many of the original deer had died. Others had been slaughtered indiscriminately for meat, killed by bears and wolves, or been stolen, or simply wandered off, never to be seen again. Yet clearly some had survived, like this herd.

A few things still puzzled him. He understood that most of the deer herds had been established on mission stations near the coast. What was this Siberian doing with his own herd, so far inland? The obvious answer was that he had stolen them. But that, thought Carver, was no concern of his. Or was it? Perhaps he should have let the Siberian drown. But then the herd was no use to him except as a supply of meat. He decided to risk further questioning.

'So what are you doing in this neck of the woods?' he demanded. 'And why were you fishing in that there creek?'

20

Abner sighed heavily. 'Many bad things happened. The missionary took sick of a fever, and finally died. Then the people began to quarrel, some saying the deer should be killed for food, others that they should be saved. Then people came from another village and tried to steal the herds. There was much fighting, and one man was killed.'

He gave a short bark of laughter. 'The Reverend Montgomery taught me I should love my neighbour as myself, but there isn't a lot of time for loving when that man is trying to stick a knife in your gut. I had been promised, once I had taught the people how to care for their reindeer, that I could have sixty animals of my own, but when I reminded the village elders of this pledge they shook their heads and said they knew nothing of such a promise.

'Quietly, I made preparations to leave the village, and one night, when the people were holding a great dance and feast, for which they had killed several deer, I cut sixty animals from the herd and drove them as far away as I could get. I kept going, until I was sure I would not be pursued. Now I'm heading north.'

'North,' echoed Carver.

Abner nodded. 'At least I was. I heard there was a land there far to the north–east, that the white traders have not yet found. This land is rich in furs, richer than any man dreamed of. Bear and wolf, mink and otter and fox and marten. There the fur bearers grow bigger, and because of the intense cold their pelts are longer and thicker, more glossy and luxuriant than they do down here in the south. The natives there are willing to trade for meat, for the caribou herds are almost all gone, and they have nothing but meat from the sea.'

Carver felt a faint stir of interest, but common sense told him that this was just another of those yarns told around camp fires. 'How do you know this place exists?' he asked.

'The man I spoke to had some silver fox for sale. When I held them at arm's length, the tails brushed the ground.'

Carver was impressed, but doubt still remained. 'Have you any idea how far it is to the north of this land?' he queried.

Slowly, Abner shook his head. 'No. Have you?'

Carver sucked thoughtfully on his pipe. Truth to tell, he didn't know either, but he guessed it was a very long way. 'It must be all of five hundred miles,' he ventured, 'but that's as the crow flies, and you ain't no crow. By the time you've driven that herd round every mountain and hill, past every muskeg swamp and river, you'll have to double the distance.'

'I'm in no hurry,' Abner replied.

'But,' Carver protested, 'have you any idea what the winters are like up there? The sun never rises for months at a time, and the wind can freeze a man's breath solid in his lungs.'

'I am a Chukchi,' said Abner with a certain hint of pride. 'And I come from the northernmost tip of Siberia. There is nowhere in the world colder than there.'

Another thought struck Carver. 'Won't your reindeer want to move south in winter, like the caribou?'

Abner shook his head. 'Reindeer have been domesticated for so long they have lost the urge to migrate. True they need some shelter in winter, but they can always find food under the snow. They will roam far in summer, seeking escape from the heat and the flies, but they always drift up wind, so they are easy to find.'

Carver had been studying the herd. 'They good stock?' he queried, waving his pipe in the direction of the deer.

The other man nodded. Carver sat silent, chewing on his pipestem. This Chukchi was honest, at least. He could have stolen the entire herd, and left the villagers to starve. The deer looked fat and sleek, though Carver now realized

KING OF THE WILD

Ewan Clarkson

CENTURY

LONDON SYDNEY AUCKLAND JOHANNESBURG

The right of Ewan Clarkson to be identified as the author of
this work has been asserted by him in accordance with the
Copyright, Designs and Patents Act 1988.

First published in Great Britain in 1990 by
Random Century Group
20 Vauxhall Bridge Road, London SW1V 2SA

Century Hutchinson South Africa (Pty) Ltd
PO Box 337, Bergvlei 2012, South Africa

Random Century Australia Pty Ltd
20 Alfred Street, Milsons Point, Sydney, NSW 2061
Australia

Random Century New Zealand Ltd
PO Box 40–086, Glenfield, Auckland 10
New Zealand

British Library Cataloguing in Publication Data
Clarkson, Ewan
King of the Wild.
I. Title
823′ .914 [F]

ISBN 0–7126–3003–1
Typeset by Selectmove Ltd, London
Printed and bound in Great Britain by
Mackays of Chatham PLC, Chatham, Kent

3

The Partnership

All that day Carver tried to dismiss Abner and his venture from his mind, but always he kept seeing a recurring vision of fox pelts that were almost as long as a man was tall. Later, as he sat by his fire, smoking a last pipe before bedding down for the night, he fell once more to pondering the plight of the reindeer herder, and the future of such an enterprise in the Arctic wilderness.

He had journeyed some twenty miles that day, his eyes constantly scanning the freshly fallen snow for signs of fur-bearing animals. What little he had seen confirmed his belief that for the time being, at any rate, the land was hunted out. He had seen a few tracks of fox, overlaying those of snowshoe hair, some porcupine, and once, evidence of a wolf pack. He had seen no sign of lynx nor otter, no marten nor mink. Once he had taken a shot at a wolverine, but he had missed, and decided not to waste further bullets on a pelt that was not in very great demand.

Given time, he was sure, the fur bearers and the larger game would renew their numbers. Until then the natives who depended upon them for food would have to survive as best they could. Meantime more and more white men were moving into the territory, fur trappers like himself, gold miners, prospectors and hunters. Behind them, as soon as the ice broke in the spring, boats from Seattle plied the northern seas and penetrated far up the rivers, bringing with them the trappings of civilization and the dregs of human society. Whole cities sprang up almost overnight, first of canvas, then of board, populated by they were slightly smaller than the wild caribou with which he was familiar.

'You'll be a rich man one day,' he observed.

'Perhaps,' said Abner sadly, 'but not for many years yet. I have no bulls. I brought three. One was killed by wolves. One fell over a cliff and broke its neck. The third –' he gestured with his hand – 'is somewhere down there under the ice. I was trying to save it when you arrived. Next year I shall have calves, but not the next year nor the next. Not until I can raise more bulls. By then the cows will be getting old, with no young stock to follow.'

Carver pondered this predicament for a moment. 'No wonder you were looking depressed back there. Can't you go back to the village and get some more?'

Abner shrugged. 'It's a long way to go just to get myself killed. Anyway, I was too greedy. I took the three best bulls.'

His clothes were dry. Carver waited long enough to retrieve his moose-hide robe, and then shook out his whip. 'Well, times a'passing,' he observed cheerfully. 'If I come across any reindeer bulls, I'll let you know.'

'Or caribou bulls,' called Abner.

Carver paused in the act of leaving. 'They interbreed then?' he asked.

'Of course,' replied Abner. 'They're the same beast, almost.'

'I didn't know that,' said Carver, musing.

He cracked his whip and the team moved away. On the plain the wind had packed the snow down hard and the going was good. Soon Abner and his deer were mere specks in the vast white bowl of the wilderness.

night. In the morning he would head over the mountains, where there lay thousands of square miles of wilderness which in all probability had never been trapped since the beginning of time. Relieved to have set his mind at rest he stomped off through the snow to collect Handsome.

Next morning he harnessed up his sledge as usual, but instead of setting out for the mountains as he had intended, he turned about and began to retrace his journey of the day before. The herd had gone from the valley in which he had left it, but the trail through the hills was easy to follow.

He found the deer just as dusk was falling, and he also found himself looking into the muzzle of a gun, an ancient flintlock of the sort supplied as a trade gun by the Hudson's Bay Company a century ago. Carver regarded it with a mixture of awe and contempt.

'Does that thing fire?' he asked.

'Sometimes,' said Abner cheerfully. 'I killed a moose with it the other week.'

'Did you now,' said Carver, impressed. 'Well, put it away before you kill me. I've got a proposition to put to you, and I can't talk with my head blown off.'

The herder's tent was a low domed structure set in the shelter of a small grove of trees, covered on the outside with a thick layer of insulating snow. Inside Carver saw it was constructed from a circle of thin willow and poplar saplings, bent and tied in the centre, and overlaid with moose-hides with the hair turned in. The floor was covered in fresh spruce branches. There was no stove, or heating of any kind, but a low bench was piled high with soft reindeer hides, and a section of moose-hide, untanned and stiff as a board, made a snug-fitting door.

Outside a fire burned red, and a section of moose rib was grilling on the coals. Beside the meat a heavy iron pot simmered gently, and a fragrant smell of soup filled the air. Carver gazed about him approvingly.

a motley crew of gamblers, confidence trickster, whores, criminals and footloose adventurers of every age, colour and sex.

There were no farmers. A man couldn't raise beef here, nor sheep nor hogs nor corn, any more than he could raise bananas. He could raise reindeer though, to sell to the natives for furs, and if they couldn't find the pelts with which to pay there were always the miners, who could pay with gold.

A man could stay, and make a rich living out of the growing population here in the south. It occurred to him that it would cost a small fortune to deliver a shipment of beef to one of the mining towns that were proliferating throughout the territory, yet whatever the cost, it would pay, for the miners would part with every ounce of their gold rather than starve. A man could supply reindeer meat at a fraction of the cost, and yet still ask a high price.

Or a man could head north, stay ahead of the game, and gamble on making an even greater fortune. Always in the past the first comers had gained the most. Sooner or later the others, the miners and prospectors, would follow, and in the meantime he could still get rich trading in furs. It occurred to him that there was nothing to stop him setting off in search of this fabled land for himself. Yet the wilderness was vast, immeasurable, and he might search for a lifetime without ever discovering the region. He wondered if the Chukchi knew the way.

The idea of trading meat for gold was attractive, but trading meat for fur, which could be converted into gold, had even greater appeal, especially as it would be supplemented by the harvest from his own traplines. Yet there seemed little future in the herd belonging to Abner. Even if there were, Carter had no knowledge of how to manage reindeer, and no money with which he could buy himself a partnership. Suddenly exasperated with his thoughts he rose to his feet and made up the fire for the

'How do you carry your fixings?' he asked.

Abner produced two bowls fashioned from birch wood, and spoons carved out of horn. 'Reindeer make good pack animals,' he answered. 'Carry ninety pounds each. Pull a sled too.'

Before he would eat, Carver insisted on seeing to his dogs and setting up his own camp in a clearing nearby. Consequently, by the time the rib bones were picked clean and water was boiling ready for tea the night was completely dark. Stars, white and lustrous, glowed in the cloudless sky and though the faces of the men were red from the heat of the fire, frost clawed at their backs as the temperature fell. Around them the silence of the wilderness descended like a shroud. Carver lit his pipe with a burning brand and smoked meditatively for a while.

At length he said, 'Do you know the way to this promised land of yours?'

Abner was silent for a while, then he said cautiously, 'My informant told me to follow certain rivers that flowed from the north-east. These would lead me to a range of high mountains that straddle the land. Beyond these there are no more mountains, only a great plain, and a wide river that flows to a frozen sea. I shall know when I've found it.'

Now it was Carver's turn to pause for reflection as he weighed the value of Abner's information against the commitment he was about to make. At last he asked, 'If I told you I knew where we could get some wild caribou bulls, could you catch them and tame them?'

Abner thought for a moment. 'If I could get close enough, I could lasso one,' he answered. 'My people, when they wanted to catch a wild reindeer bull, used to use a tame bull, fitted with a cage made out of antlers. When the wild bull saw the tame one, he would attack, and get his antlers tangled up in the cage, but, as you

27

know, we have no bulls. As for taming one, well, you can never completely tame even a reindeer bull, but you can get him used to you. Do you think you could find one?'

'Maybe,' said Carver. 'There are some people I know, the Nunamiut. They are Eskimos, but they don't live on the coast. They live inland, somewhere away to the north, and they live off the caribou. Those deer provide everything they need, food and tents and clothing, even weapons. They wander about a lot, never stay for very long in one spot, but if anyone can find deer, they can.'

'Can you find these people though, if they are always on the move?'

'No need to go looking,' said Carver. 'Come the spring, I know just where they will be, waiting for the deer to go by on their migration north. All we have to do is to turn up there, and wait for the people and the deer to arrive.' He did not feel it necessary to add that the success of the suggestion depended on the hope that sufficient caribou still survived, and that the Nunamiut had not been starved out of existence. 'In return for my help,' he added, 'I'd want an interest in the herd.'

'Of course,' agreed Abner. 'I'm already deeply in your debt. You saved my life, remember. Equal shares.'

During the next few weeks the two men drifted steadily north, averaging five to fifteen miles a day depending on the weather, with frequent halts to allow the deer to graze. Carver stayed loosely attached, sometimes journeying on ahead, or, when he found a pocket of fur bearers, lingering behind while he added to his meagre store of pelts. Supplies of food, for both men and dogs, were running low. Fortunately moose were plentiful in the willow thickets that flourished along the creeks, and from time to time the report of Carver's heavy Lee Metford rifle would echo and roll among the hills. Then there would be moose tongue

28

and liver for supper, and the dogs would gorge until they could eat no more.

Towards the end of the third week they had begun to climb high into the hills, and Carver knew by the outline of the mountains looming over them that they were nearing their goal. Now he began to cast about, searching for a safe refuge, somewhere the deer could graze where they were unlikely to be discovered.

'Best to be on the safe side,' he explained to Abner. 'As I remember, these Nanamiut were a pretty timid, biddable lot, but their ideas about property and ownership don't always exactly square with ours. They won't see these deer as anything else but meat, and if they get to thinking, they'll want us to share the whole lot. By far the best if they don't know the deer exist.'

They found what they sought, in an upland meadow bounded by precipitous cliffs, where once, aeons ago, a glacier had ground its ponderous way. Here the land was well drained, and under the snow lay a luxuriant mat of grasses and lichens, enough browse to last the deer for several weeks. They set up camp at the entrance to the valley, where a grove of aspen and poplar bordered a small stream. From here Abner commanded a good view of the land that sloped away to the south, so he would have plenty of warning in the unlikely event of a visit by strangers.

Early next morning Carver set off in search of the elusive nomads. He travelled light, taking only the minimum of supplies to sustain him. Spring was fast approaching. The days were growing visibly longer, and at noon the temperature sometimes rose above freezing. Then the snow grew sticky and soft, making hard work for the dogs, balling beneath their pads and forming gobbets of ice between their toes. At night the temperature fell again, and in the mornings the snow bore a hard crust of glaze. If the crust was thick enough to bear the weight of the team, progress was swift, but sometimes it was so thin that the

29

dogs broke through at every step, cutting their feet and legs.

More and more Carver was beginning to see the advantages that reindeer had over dogs. They could be used as pack animals, or ridden, and even one of the cows could pull a sledge laden with two men. Harnessed in tandem they could pull a great deal more, and their broad hooves supported their weight equally well in deep snow or on frozen crust. Unlike dogs, they did not have to carry their own supply of food. In fact they were a supply of meat in themselves. In dire emergency a man could always eat his dogs, but reindeer meat was far nicer.

All that day he travelled higher and higher into the hills, heading towards a saddle between two peaks. By evening he stood just below the pass, looking down from a low ridge on a trail that stretched away to the north. It was a broad trail, and in places where the snow had been blown away by the wind, Carver could see how the very rock itself had been worn away, rutted over the millennia by the passage of countless hooves. He had reached the migration route of the caribou. Just beyond the ridge, he knew, lay the place where each spring and autumn the Nunamiut came to harvest the deer.

He found them next morning, camped in a snug dry hollow on the northern slope of the hills, their low domed tents of caribou hide looking like a herd of giant tortoises that had come to rest in the snow. They ran to meet him as he approached, some twenty men, women and children, laughing and chattering excitedly as they gathered around, fingering his robes and the long knife that hung at his belt, combing his beard with questing fingers and giggling at the feel of it. They remember me, thought Carver, and was glad about it. He was thankful too that he had been prudent enough to leave his sledge and dogs behind. The first time he had met them they had stripped the sledge of all his belongings, and it had taken him two days, and much cajoling, to get his property back.

One person stood apart, a seemingly round butterball of a man, bundled in furs, his greasy face split in a huge grin. This was Heyhok, the leader. Carver knew that his appearance of obesity was an illusion, and that in reality Heyhok was all muscle, squat and thick-necked, and renowned for his skill as a wrestler. The two men embraced, Carver holding his breath against the stench of decaying teeth and rotten meat that hung around the Nunamiut. Then, delving in his parka, Carver produced presents of tobacco, tea and sugar, gifts that he knew were most likely to win their way to Heyhok's heart.

Heyhok shouted with glee and held his trophies aloft. Then at his command two women scurried away and returned with an enormous iron pot they had at some time acquired. Others came bearing armfuls of dry wood, and Carver wondered how many miles they had walked to collect so much. Now it seemed they were about to squander a week's firewood in one reckless blaze.

The pot, packed with snow, was set among the flames, and barely had the snow melted than bloody, unrecognizable chunks of meat were thrown in. Then, as everyone sat around, waiting expectantly for the whole mess to boil, the questioning began: Where Had Carver come from? How had the hunting been? Was the quality of the pelts up to standard?

Carver answered each question slowly and patiently. He had a good working knowledge of both the Eskimo tongues spoken in the region, but he had long ago learned to pretend he understood less than he did. That way he learned more, and revealed less, all the while confirming the natives' conviction that all white men were stupid. The one question everyone wanted to ask hung unspoken round the fire. It would be the height of discourtesy for anyone to

31

ask Carver why it was he came visiting until after he had been fed.

At last the meat was deemed ready, though in truth it was barely half-cooked. Carver took the proffered portion and surreptitiously scraped away as much of the hair still adhering as he could. The meat was tough and tasteless, impossible to bite. Carver had to eat Eskimo fashion, sinking his teeth into a morsel of meat and trimming off the surplus that protruded from his lips with his knife. He chewed slowly, hoping his digestion would not suffer too early in the proceedings. All around him grimy hands clawed for the other portions, which were washed down with the thin soup in which the meat had boiled.

When that was all gone, tea was brewed, black, sweet, and strong enough to cause palpitations. Since no one had bothered to wash the pot, the surface of the brew was clotted with fat globules and stray deer hairs, together with a flotsam of twigs and leaves that had been picked up with the snow. Heyhok drank about a pint, belched contentedly, and voiced the thought that had been uppermost in his mind ever since Carver had arrived.

'So! Now you are here, you will kill many deer for us.'

Carver thought for a moment. 'The deer are thin. There is no meat on their bones, and no fat in their flesh. They are shedding their hair, and the hides are full of holes from warble flies. Better surely to kill them in the fall, when they are sleek and fat?'

The big man sighed patiently. 'Meat's meat to a hungry man, no matter how lean and stringy. But it is not meat we seek at the moment. Now is the time the cows carry calves, and the skin of the unborn calf serves many purposes. It makes clothing for children, and undergarments for men and women. Besides, the cows provide leg skins for boots, and though their hides are poor, they are good enough for tent skins. As for the meat, it will not be wasted.'

32

Carver nodded. 'If I do this for you, will you in turn help me?'

Heyhok flung an arm around his shoulder. 'Surely. We are friends, are we not? And what are friends for, if not to help each other? Stay with us, and kill deer, and I will give you all the help you need.'

'I cannot stay now,' said Carver. 'Back there, beyond the mountains, a great shaman waits. He sends me to do his bidding. He needs young caribou bulls, captured alive and unharmed.'

Heyhok shifted uneasily, and his anxiety was reflected in a ripple of murmured awe from the circle of listeners. No man cared to involve himself with a shaman if he could avoid it. Their magic was strong, and while they could cure disease, find game or even kill an enemy if need be, the payment they exacted was inclined to be heavy.

'What would a shaman want with live deer?' Heyhok queried.

'Who is the greater fool?' asked Carver. 'He who questions a shaman's ways, or he who refuses to do his bidding?'

Heyhok, who had no wish to be any kind of fool, could only reiterate his promise of help, but the feeling of happiness, which had warmed him like a sun, had been replaced by the bitter chill of fear. He wished now that he had not been so eager to ask Carver to kill deer, but he had wanted to show his people he was a man who could persuade anyone to do his bidding, and the opportunity had seemed too good to miss. It was too late to change his mind. Already the white man was preparing to take his leave. Now Heyhok hoped he would not return, and so absolve him from his promise.

Carver did return however, only two days later, and this time he stayed with the Nunamiut until the day dawned when the lookouts posted by Heyhok came racing down the hill with the news that the deer were coming. With a sigh Carver loaded his rifle and took up his position behind a low outcrop of rock, overlooking the trail along which the deer would pass.

The range was no more than a hundred yards, and the sun was at his back. At first it was very quiet in the still Arctic air, and then he heard a low rumble, like the growl of distant thunder, a far drumming that resolved itself into a loud cacophony, a clicking of tendons and a chorus of bleats and grunts, overlaid by the din of countless hooves. As the leading cows came abreast of him he took careful aim and fired.

The heavy Lee Metford bucked and kicked, and at the sound of the report a caribou cow crumpled at the knees and pitched sideways, her hooves flailing the snow as if she were impatient to get up and resume her journey north again. Around her the rest of the herd, as heedless of her fate as they had been of the rifle shot, continued on their relentless way.

Carver ejected the spent round from the breech. It fell into a snow drift, from which it was instantly retrieved by one of the children. Carver ignored the child, took aim, and fired again. The killing did not take long, and at the end of it he lowered the rifle and stood up, ruefully massaging his shoulder. He was sore in spirit as well as in body. He had no objection to killing, for meat or for hide, but this slaughter sickened him.

This must have been how it was in the days of the buffalo skinners, when men sat for hours firing a heavy Sharp's rifle into the herd, dropping beast after beast until the barrel of the rifle grew red hot. Then the skinners moved in, taking only the tongues and hides, and leaving the carcases to rot in the hot prairie sun. Sometimes, it was said, when the skinners were working up wind, it took a whole day to ride clear of the stench.

34

By contrast this was a modest kill, but the same smell of blood and offal hung on the still air, and Carver wanted no more part of it. He shouldered his rifle and wandered away uphill, where he sat smoking his pipe and watching the Nunamiut as they went about their work.

Around him the tundra was littered with carcases, some still intact, others without a hide and steaming in the cold air. More were in various stages of dismemberment. Long strips of meat were laid out on the rocks to dry, guarded from the ravens by squealing, shouting children, some toddlers barely able to walk. The women were bent over the hides, and the men were butchering and skinning yet more. All were in festive mood, laughing and joking with each other as they worked, their hands and faces stained with blood, the fur on their parkas matted and foul. The numbers of the caribou passing through were growing fewer now, the herds smaller and less frequent. Soon the bulls would be coming along, and it was time for him to go and collect Abner.

The tall Siberian had looked a little anxious when Carver had told him he was to play the part of a shaman, though Carver had assured him that the Nunamiut were unlikely to challenge his status. For his part Carver was more concerned about the fate of the reindeer herd, which would be left free to wander where it pleased, unguarded from wolf or bear. Abner seemed curiously fatalistic about this, merely saying that they would not wander far, and that in any case his herd dogs would find them, wherever they had strayed.

Early next morning Carver harnessed up his team and set off to make the short journey to the valley where the reindeer herd was gathered. For a while the going was good, but as the sun rose higher in the sky the snow began to melt, sticking to the runners of the sledge and slowing the dogs down. In places the snow had completely gone, and the stony surface of the ground tore at the runners of his sledge as it rattled and bounced along. Carver drove his dogs hard, using his whip with unaccustomed vigour. Another few days and the snow would be all gone, and the sledge would be virtually useless.

He had further cause to hurry. Now that the nomads had a plentiful supply of meat, he could not guarantee they would linger long, and he did not want them to disappear into the vast emptiness of the tundra without fulfilling their part of the bargain. He thought it unlikely. They had plenty of work to do, and more meat than they could possibly carry. Lacking any sort of sledge, they had only a few small dogs to carry their loads, and the backs of their women, who were usually bent double with the weight of their tents and sleeping robes. All the same he resolved to return that night, when the ground would be frozen and the snow firm.

Fifty miles to the south Anak lifted his muzzle to the breeze that blew down from the hills. Two hundred miles of his journey lay behind him, and he was eager to be on the move once more. He had enjoyed two good winters since the summer of his birth, and despite the long hours of darkness, the bitter chill of the freezing nights and the deep snow that blanketed the vegetation he had fed tolerably well. There was nourishment in plenty to be gained from slender shoots of willow and aspen, poplar and birch, along with the evergreen fronds of cedar.

Already he commanded respect from the companions of his calfhood. From an early age he had learned to use his extra bulk and weight to gain advantage over others of his age group. A sudden shoulder charge would carry him from the outskirts of the herd into the centre, where he was sheltered from the worst bite of the wind, and protected from the predators which from time to time menaced the deer. His antlers, though they had yet to develop the full sweep and majesty of those possessed by some of the older bulls, were still potent weapons. One wicked sideways sweep was enough to warn away any other who sought to trespass too close.

For a while longer he grazed on the moss and withered grass, scraping away the thin layer of snow with his forelegs and snatching each mouthful as it was exposed. Then, suddenly, he gave an impatient snort and ran to the front of the herd, pushing aside those deer who stood in his way. The ripple of movement so started spread rapidly among the herd, and within seconds the deer were on the move once more. The day's trek had begun.

Away to the north, Carver and Abner stood by as the Nunamiut, with boundless energy and enthusiasm, set about preparing for a traditional hunt. A few miles distant from the camp the trail followed by the migrating caribou sloped gradually down into a broad vale. At first the slopes of the surrounding hills were curved and gentle, but a little way into the valley the sides grew steeper, until the trail was bordered by precipitous cliffs. These in turn ended abruptly, giving way to sloping hills once more, but away to the left was a narrow gorge or cleft, twisting and worming its way into the hills.

This terminated in a natural amphitheatre, from which there was no easy exit. In late summer the floor of this arena was a waterlogged meadow of moss and luxuriant grass. Now, in the spring thaw, it was a shallow lake of melting snow and rotten, honeycombed ice. This was one of the traditional killing grounds of the Nunamiut, into which each year for untold centuries they had driven the deer, before sealing off the entrance and slaughtering the herd.

Across the valley floor at the entrance to the gorge stood a curving row of stone columns, each about twenty feet apart, and standing the height of a man. The work of restoring these columns was well in hand; any stones that

37

had fallen off were replaced and each column topped with a thatch of dried grass and moss. Thus adorned, they looked remarkably lifelike, but as yet there were plenty of wide gaps, through which the deer could easily pass.

Watching the people, hearing their shouts and laughter as they worked, Carver realized that his fears of the Nunamiut failing to fill their side of the bargain were groundless.

'There's an old saying,' he remarked to Abner. 'An Indian hunts to live, but an Eskimo lives to hunt. It's as true as I'm standing here. Look at them. Happy as fleas on a dog's back.'

'All except one,' remarked Abner. 'Maybe he's an Indian.' He jerked his head in the direction of one individual who stood alone on the edge of the crowd. He was a tall youth, fast approaching manhood, but though he appeared willing and eager enough to help, he seemed unsure of what was expected of him.

'Maybe he's a bit weak in the head,' observed Carver.

At last it seemed the work was almost done. The nomads sat or laid around on the sun-warmed rocks that now stood clear of snow.

'What happens next?' asked Abner.

Carver pointed back along the trail, to where a solitary figure stood outlined against the sky. 'Heyhok is waiting for the deer. When he sees them he will come running back down the trail in time for everyone to get into position. After that things are liable to happen rather fast. Are you ready?'

Abner shrugged. 'As ready as I will ever be, I suppose.'

Carver eyed him, and grinned. 'You look like a parcel that's coming untied.'

The tall Siberian did indeed have a curious appearance. Two rawhide lariats, each about fifty feet long, hung coiled across his chest, bandolier fashion. Shorter lengths of cord hung festooned from his belt and trailed almost to the ground, so that he appeared to be wearing a grass skirt.

'We'd best hide ourselves away,' observed Carver. 'The deer catch a sight of you looking like that, they're going to stampede in all directions.'

Together the two men made their way slantwise across the side of the hill, to where an outcrop of grey weathered rock hid them from view and gave shelter from the chill breeze that blew down from the snow fields higher up the hill. There they lit their pipes and settled down to wait.

The long hours passed. The sun rolled slowly towards the south, maintaining station just above the horizon. The silence was so profound that the croak of a solitary raven soaring black-winged over the hills made both men jump. From somewhere under the snow a tiny rivulet of melt water started to flow, and the musical trickle of water seemed to beat at long-drawn-out intervals, like the slow pulse of the living earth. Carver was drifting off to sleep when a sudden exclamation from Abner roused him.

High on the hill a tiny figure was frantically waving its arms, signalling a wild semaphore to those waiting below. Then it disappeared from view as Heyhok left the skyline and began running towards them, appearing again from time to time silhouetted against a snow field. Abner glanced away, looking back to where the people a moment ago were lying about in the sun, but they had vanished without trace.

Now there was nothing they could do but hope, until Heyhok arrived, sweating profusely and blowing hard, to join them in the shelter of the outcrop.

'You smell like a long dead grizzly,' remarked Carver conversationally, in English.

Heyhok nodded and smiled happily. 'They come. Small herd. Young bulls, just as you wanted.' He seemed as pleased as if he had personally organized the delivery.

Long minutes passed as Carver strained his eyes for the first sight of the deer. The sun glare bouncing off the snow fields made him blink, and he wished he had thought to wear goggles. Then he saw them, like a swarm of large black bees moving steadily downhill. They grew bigger, and soon he could make out the forest of antlers, a delicate intertracery of twigs that seemed to float above the herd. Then it was upon them, sweeping inexorably past, and at that moment Heyhok, who had been holding his breath with pent-up excitement, let out a long-drawn howl.

At his signal the people materialized as if by magic from the emptiness of the tundra where they had lain hidden, concealed under the raw caribou hides. Advancing in line, holding the hides between them like blankets, they formed a living wall between the stone sentinels, swinging round in a great arc so that it seemed to the oncoming deer that the gap ahead was slowly closing. The manoeuvre was so perfectly executed that the leading caribou instinctively swerved to the left and then, as they faltered, hesitating before plunging into the gorge, Heyhok rushed out of hiding and appeared behind the herd, stampeding it with wild yells and waving arms.

In the centre of the milling throng Anak snorted with mingled fear and rage as he was swept along, jostled and buffeted by others in the herd. He tried to slow down, but the press from the back was such that he was in danger of being overthrown and trampled underfoot. Beside him one deer did go down, to lie thrashing and kicking as others tried to leap over it. Then they were through the gorge and the pressures eased as the caribou splashed into the icy snow broth that floated on top of the lake.

The waters were not deep, no more than five feet at the deepest part, but the deer were forced to swim, milling in circles as the Nunamiut surrounded the lake. Anak struck out for the far shore, separating himself from others in the herd, and as he did so a black snake flickered out over him and caressed his shoulder before sliding back into the water. It came a second time, entwining itself in his antlers, and next moment Anak felt a sudden jerk.

He reared up in the water, shaking his head in a welter of foam as he tried to free himself, and at the other end of the lasso Abner felt himself pulled waist deep into the water. Another moment and he would have been dragged off his feet, but just then an extra pair of strong hands gripped the thin rawhide and another pair of shoulders leaned on the rope. At first Abner thought it was Carver come to his aid, but when he risked a glance he saw to his surprise that it was none other than the young Eskimo he had observed earlier in the day.

Gone was the youth's earlier irresolution. He seemed to know exactly what he was doing, giving line when the deer pulled too strongly, backing up and gaining ground whenever the beast weakened. Together they hauled it out on to the shore, and now Carver lent his wiry strength to the tug of war, hanging on to the rope while Abner worked his way hand over hand to the deer's head.

Now he seized the caribou by the base of the antlers, and by twisting the head sideways and throwing his whole weight against the animal, Abner was able to fling it down on its side. Twisting like an eel, he laid across the shoulder, and drew one of the strings from his belt. With a speed and dexterity born of long practice, he roped first the forelegs, then the hind. In less than a minute Anak lay trussed and helpless by the lake.

Scarcely pausing for breath Abner uncoiled his other lariat, and after a few attempts succeeded in roping another promising young bull. Once again the strange youth was immediately at his side, helping to subdue the struggling animal, while Carver retrieved and coiled the first lariat. This time the boy darted in and secured the legs of the captive, almost as proficiently as Abner had done.

41

In a remarkably short time a third bull lay prisoner, and the three men collapsed exhausted beside the lake. It was fortunate for them that they had not delayed too long in securing their prizes. The Nunamiut, until now held in check by Heyhok, were wild with excitement at the sight of so much meat, and had already begun to use their copper-tipped spears with deadly effect. The melting snow broth foamed scarlet and pink. Carcases floated belly up, and were trampled underfoot as the maddened deer tried to escape. None succeeded. As the last deer died the people began hauling the bodies from the water.

Carver turned to the young man who had helped them capture the deer, asking him how he had acquired his skill, but the boy only stared at him blankly. Carver repeated the question and then, as a sudden suspicion formed in his mind, asked him again. This time he spoke in Yupik rather than Inupiaq, the language the nomads used. At once the light of comprehension dawned in the youth's eyes and he began to speak, at first hesitantly, and then, as his excitement grew, in a torrent of words so fast that Carver held up his hands in protest, begging him to slow down. At long last Carver turned to Abner.

'Seems he's some sort of foundling, a stray the Nunamiut picked up in their wanderings. He has no family, and no friends. His name is Ootek, and he's from the coast somewhere away to the north. His family were starving, so they set off to walk inland in search of game. One by one they died of starvation, but he managed to survive by catching and eating the ravens that came to feed on the corpses of his parents. Then the Nunamiut found him and took him in. He's not happy, though. He can hardly speak their language, nor does he understand their ways. Says he wants to go back north, to the sea, to find others of his own kind.'

To Carver's surprise Abner merely nodded. 'The language he speaks is very much like that of my own people, though his accent is strange.' Turning to the boy he asked, 'Where did you learn to rope a deer?'

Ootek laughed. 'I didn't, but hauling a deer out of a swamp is no different to pulling a harpooned seal or walrus out from under a hole in the ice. In fact I think it is easier.'

Abner ruefully swung his aching arms. 'Then I hope I never have to haul in a walrus,' he commented. 'Why don't we take him along with us?' he asked Carver, speaking now in English. 'We are heading in the direction he wants to go, and we could use an extra hand getting these back to the herd.'

Carver considered for a moment. It was true they could do with some help transporting the deer. After that the boy could stay with them, or go his own way.

'Better check with Heyhok,' he said cautiously. 'We don't want to cause any bad feeling at this stage.'

He needn't have worried. Heyhok seemed vastly relieved to be rid of someone who had proved to be something of a misfit, and genuinely pleased that events had turned out so well. Ootek was overjoyed at the invitation, and as the Nunamiut busied themselves harvesting their meat, the three set about the task of transporting the bulls across country to the waiting reindeer cows.

4

Wild Bull

The journey back to the valley was one that none of them were likely to forget. It was Abner's first experience in dealing with wild caribou, and he had assumed they were little different from the semi-tame reindeer to which he was accustomed. He was soon to find he was mistaken.

He had made rawhide halters for each of the three bulls, and it was a comparatively easy matter to fit these as the animals lay hogtied on the ground. Each halter was joined by a connecting lead about five feet long. Abner's plan was to hobble the bulls with loose cords tied to their forelegs, and to lead them abreast across the tundra, with the big bull, Anak, in the centre and the two smaller ones on either side. He and Ootek would walk between the bulls, holding on to their antlers. Carver was to follow behind with the sledge.

Anak's first paroxysm of fear had passed, and finding he was powerless to break the ties that held him fast he ceased to struggle, and lay passively on his side in the snow. The moment Carver untied the knots however, and Anak felt his legs freed, he sprang to his feet and tried to gallop away, only to trip on his hobbles and fall, dragging Abner on top of him. Still grimly hanging on to his antlers, Abner hauled Anak to his feet, where he stood trembling and quiescent, but facing the wrong way. Quickly Carver untied the other two, and for the next half hour the three men struggled vainly to untangle the bucking, fighting deer. At length, when hobbles, traces and antlers were entwined in an inextricable knot, Abner dived in among the flailing hooves, and after a considerable

buffeting managed to retie the bulls so that they couldn't move. Then he cut the connecting ropes and sat back, for the moment defeated.

There was no alternative but to load the bulls on to the sledge and transport them with the dogs. Each bull weighed around three hundred pounds, making a heavy load even when the terrain was flat and snow conditions good. The way back to the valley lay across low hills, and the thaw was already well advanced. Fortunately the dogs were well rested and eager to work again, but time after time the sledge runners stuck in the wet snow, or ground to a halt on bare earth.

After a few miles Carver stopped his team and fitted each dog with the protective boots he carried for that purpose. He was not too soon. Already some of the dogs had cut and bleeding pads where ice crystals and sharp rocks had cut through the tough skin. Ootek and Abner took their place at the head of the team, adding their strength to that of the dogs, but even so progress was slow.

Anak was securely tied to the sledge, but was still continually buffeted and shaken. Fear returned, and the thudding of his heart against his ribs was like a drum beat that echoed through his brain. Unable to see where he was going, or to hear any sound above the creaking and groaning of the sledge, and the wild shrieks of the runners as they scraped over the ground, Anak gradually drifted into a stupor, so that he was only dimly aware of the passage of time.

The sledge alternately ground to a halt or jerked forward with a jolt that time and again brought Carver to his knees. At intervals he was forced to call a halt to adjust the lashings, and then men and dogs had to strain to the utmost to get the sledge moving again.

The early sun had given way to threatening low clouds, and as the wind increased in strength it became noticeably colder. Despite this all three men were sweating freely.

Carver's arms ached from wrestling with the handles of the sledge as he tried in vain to guide it round the worst of the bumps, and the rawhide bit into the shoulders of the other men as they leaned into the ropes.

Snow began to fall, first in stinging white needles, which as the wind increased merged into a feathery white blanket blowing horizontally against their faces, covering the deer as they lay helpless and suffering on the sledge. Progress became slower and slower as men and dogs grew weaker, but the thin covering of freshly fallen snow made the sledge run a little easier. At last, as night was falling and the wind howled in fury over the hills, they heard the frenzied barking of Abner's herd dogs, and knew they had reached the sanctuary of the valley.

Still there could be no rest for the three men. First the sled dogs had to be staked and fed, and the reindeer herd rounded up from the far end of the valley. Then the caribou had to be set free. They untied the leg thongs, but left the halters in place and retied the hobbles before turning the bulls loose with the cows.

At first Anak could barely stand, and when he tried to move he stumbled over the restraining hobbles. He made no attempt to escape, however – much to Abner's relief – but stood quietly, head bowed against the driving snow, and seemingly accepting the reindeer cows as part of his herd. The other two bulls stayed close to his side, and for once he did not drive them away.

Only then were the three men able to attend to their own needs, to kindle a fire and grill some of the fresh caribou meat Carver had thought to bring with him from the morning's kill. His last thought, as he wrapped himself in his robes and drifted off to sleep, was that he never wanted to drive a dog team again.

By morning the spring snow storm had blown itself out, and blue sky, flecked with fleecy white clouds, replaced the lowering skies of the night before. Sunlight flooded

the mountain tops, staining them red and gold, while in the shadowed hollows the snow fields shone indigo and midnight blue. White pristine snow flecked with gold carpeted the valley floor, and by the stream the young leaves of the aspen shimmered pale green. The reindeer, quietly scraping away the snow to get at the lichen underneath, gave the scene a Christmas card effect. Carver, waking refreshed and lying snug beneath his robes, noted with relief that the three bulls were grazing contentedly along with the rest. As he lay drinking in the peace and beauty of the scene he reflected that a man could do worse than to end his days in such peaceful surroundings.

For a moment the dream lingered, only to be replaced by another vision, of a land far to the north and himself with a sledge laden with a mountain of pelts – thick, luxuriant, glossy – destined to clothe the richest women in the world and make him one of the wealthiest men. Suddenly impatient to begin the journey he leapt from his bed, only to discover, to his chagrin, that Abner had no intention of making such a move.

'It's out of the question,' he explained. 'The bulls need time to rest, to settle down and get used to the cows. Besides, the cows are near to calving, and once the calves are born we must wait until they are strong enough to keep up with the herd on the march. We'll spend the summer here.'

Carver fretted and fumed, but Abner would not be budged from his decision. 'This valley is as good a place as any for a calving ground. If we move now we may not find one so good.'

When Carver complained that it would be years, at this rate, before they reached their destination Abner reminded him, 'I told you I was in no hurry.'

Despite Carver's initial impatience, the short summer passed swiftly. Ironically, just as he had convinced himself that the wilderness was hunted out, he discovered he had stumbled on a corner where game was still prolific. The fur bearers were past their prime, their pelts faded and worn with the rigours of winter, but in the dense willow thickets that grew along the numerous waterways moose were plentiful, so there was no shortage of meat.

Ootek supplied the variety in their diet. Almost from the time they first set eyes on him he had proved an invaluable addition to their team. Although, when he had first joined them, he had possessed nothing more than the clothes he stood up in, he quickly acquired an outfit of his own, fashioning all the tools and weapons he required from the natural materials around him.

There were great flocks of geese and waterfowl nesting on the lakes and swamps that lay in the valley bottoms, and Ootek harvested the eggs in season. The adult birds he killed with his *killamitaun*. This was a type of bolas, made from six bone weights each attached to a cord about two foot long. The other ends of the cord were tied together in a bunch of goose quills, and when thrown by Ootek, formed a circle about four feet in diameter. When it hit the bird, the weights wrapped round its wings, bringing it to the ground. Carver tried his skill with this weapon many times, but never succeeded in making a strike. Ootek rarely missed.

His skill at setting snares was even greater, and he kept the camp regularly supplied with snowshoe hares, grouse and ptarmigan. He gathered herbs too, especially sourdock, which added its piquant flavour to soups and stews. In summer the berries ripened, and again he harvested quantities to store for the winter.

Hunting and foraging, tending to the deer herd and gathering firewood kept the three men busy most of the time. The calving season was a good one, and by July the herd had almost doubled in size. Mortalities were few, and the young calves grew at an astonishing rate. Abner spent long hours just watching them. Soon they would be strong enough to set out on their journey north. Meantime he stayed on guard against any possible threat from wolves or bears.

None came. Sometimes a solitary eagle soared overhead, alert for any calf that was sickly or had strayed too far from its dam, and on such occasions Abner fired a blast from his ancient trade gun at the bird. He never hit one, to his knowledge, but usually the warning was enough to send the eagle on its way.

Often, Ootek would join Abner in his vigil. Abner was glad of his company, and found himself growing fonder of the boy with each passing day. He also welcomed the chance to talk again in his mother tongue, which had grown rusty after years of disuse. In return he started teaching Ootek English, and found the boy quick to learn. Abner spent long hours recalling life in his village on the coast of Siberia, where the people kept vast herds of reindeer, more than any man could count, and how, each summer the people from the coast of Alaska would sail across the straits in their open skin boats to trade seal oil and skins for reindeer hides and meat.

When Ootek asked why the people of Alaska had never thought of keeping their own reindeer herds, and so saved themselves an arduous journey each year, Abner looked surprised, and then shocked.

'Oh, but they did, but never seriously. It was an event, you see, a time of great feasting and rejoicing, a chance to meet with old friends, and for the young ones perhaps a chance to marry. It was a time everyone looked forward to each year. The trading was not all that important, because everyone had everything they needed, unlike now.'

Ootek considered this in silence for a while. 'I will be glad when we reach the coast and we are able to trade reindeer meat and hides for some seal oil and whale blubber,' he mused. Another thought struck him. 'Perhaps, too, I could afford to buy myself a bride.'

Abner glanced sharply at the figure sitting beside him. The boy is becoming a man, he thought. He will not endure the solitary life in the wilderness for long. He sighed. He too missed the sea, the sight and sound and smell of it, but he knew that many months of hard travel lay between them and the particular part of the coast he sought.

The three wild bulls had settled down quietly with the herd, and showed no signs of wishing to stray. Anak was clearly recognizable even at a distance, being far and away the largest of the deer. Like the rest, he had begun to grow his new antlers, and they sprouted at an extraordinary rate, gaining an inch or so each day. From the start the big bull had held a special attraction for Ootek, and each day the boy visited him, stroking the soft silver velvet that covered his antlers and sinking his hand deep into his shaggy mane to scratch his hide. He always took some offering with him, a spray of tender aspen or willow leaves, or an armful of birch twigs, and these Anak would accept as if they were a tribute due to him, nuzzling the boy's neck and face while he was being fondled. With Abner and Carver he remained wild, unapproachable, cantering away if either of them were to approach too close.

The one flaw in this otherwise idyllic existence was the presence of the flies. They came in waves, each generation surviving about three weeks, and each seemingly bigger and stronger than the previous one. For nine weeks they attacked both deer and men, and at times they were so bad that the deer stampeded away, seeking the cool waters of the lakes or the river. The men were to some extent protected by their skin clothing, which they were forced to wear despite the heat of the Arctic summer. Their faces and hands though were attacked continually, so that at times they appeared to be wearing fur masks and gloves. Smoke from the fire brought some relief, but they were never entirely free from torment. The last sound they heard at night before they drifted off to sleep was the high-pitched

50

whine of countless mosquitoes, and it was still there in the early dawn. At such times Carver found himself longing for the first snows and the frosts that would destroy most of the insect hordes.

The bond between Anak and Ootek continued to grow. One warm lazy afternoon, when Abner and Carver were away in the hills, hunting for meat with which to replenish the larder, Anak lay almost hidden in the long grass, dozing and chewing the cud. Ootek wandered over, and leaning against the bull's shoulder began to scratch him just behind the ears. As Anak submitted to the caress Ootek slipped one leg over his back. Very slowly and tentatively, expecting any moment that Anak would lurch to his feet and tumble him in the grass, Ootek lowered his weight on to the caribou's back. Anak merely stretched out his neck and rested his muzzle on the ground, abandoning himself to the luxury of being scratched. Ootek sat there for a while, and then, just as slowly, he eased himself off the animal's back and went in search of some lengths of rawhide rope.

Anak still wore the head collar he had been fitted with on his capture, and it was a simple matter for Ootek to fit him with reins. Once more he slid his leg over the bull's back, only to find that Anak steadfastly refused to stand up. At first hesitantly, and then with increased impatience and vigour, Ootek tried every means he could think of, slapping his reluctant mount on the rump, digging his heels into Anak's flanks and pulling on the rawhide reins.

At last Anak lurched to his feet, and to Ootek's delight he actually took a few steps forward, but then he stopped and began to graze, and no amount of kicking and tugging on Ootek's part would make him lift his head. Instead, Ootek practised mounting and dismounting, an indignity Anak suffered for some little while before suddenly bucking his young rider off on to the soft turf.

Having thus discovered he could rid himself of his burden with such ease, Anak promptly threw Ootek off again the moment he remounted. Ootek however was an Eskimo, and he had learned the art of patience during the long hours he had stood in subzero temperatures, waiting for a seal to surface through the ice. He had also learned from an early age to laugh at misfortune and to persist in any endeavour. Time and again he flew through the air, and each time he bounced happily to his feet and climbed back once more. In the end his endurance proved greater than Anak's, and at last the bull accepted him without protest. Even so, it was to take more than a week before he would obey Ootek's commands, and then only when he was in a cooperative mood.

At the same time, with each succeeding day the bond between Eskimo youth and wild caribou grew stronger. At first light Anak would watch and wait for Ootek to emerge from his shelter. If Abner or Carver were also awake and moving around the camp Anak would stay away, but if Ootek was on his own Anak would come trotting over, to be greeted and fondled by the one man he was prepared to trust. Ootek, for his part, was careful to do nothing to betray that trust.

At last the first frosts came, painting the hillsides red, russet, and gold. Light showers of snow fell, mingled with hail, and the air was filled with the clamour of wild geese as they began their migration south. The deer were sleek and fat after a summer of rich grazing, and the thick shoulder capes of the bulls shone white against the darker hair of their flanks. Their antlers were full grown now, sweeping scimitar curves arching forward over their muzzles and dwarfing the smaller antlers of the cows.

As their antlers hardened and the blood supply to the velvet dwindled and finally dried up, the sensitive coating of skin began to irritate the bulls. Their tempers grew uncertain, and Abner was forced to warn Ootek of the

52

dangers of trying to be too familiar with a rutting bull. Ootek listened and nodded gravely, but an hour later Abner noticed that he was once more keeping company with the deer. Abner shrugged and said nothing. The boy had been warned, and if he couldn't learn easily, there was always the hard way.

Always dominant over the other two bulls, Anak now bullied them unmercifully, driving them away whenever they encroached too closely on his presence. He also took a dislike to one of Abner's herd dogs. One evening, as Abner was trying to isolate one of the calves, which earlier he had noticed was limping, Anak charged the dog.

Unaccustomed to such rebellious behaviour on the part of the deer the dog stood its ground, baring its teeth and snarling. When Anak did not back off and turn tail as expected of him the dog flew at his muzzle and nipped him sharply on the lip, intending to teach him manners. Anak reared back, shaking his head. Then, as the dog sprang forward to punish him further, Anak reared on his hind legs and stamped down hard.

It was all over before Abner could interfere. The dog's spine was broken in several places. Even as Abner bent to pick it up the animal's breathing became rapid and disoriented. The heart beat like a hammer against the rib cage for the space of a few seconds, and then the dog was dead.

Abner carried the limp body over to the edge of the meadow, where a patch of loose scree lay spread at the foot of the mountainside. He buried it under a cairn of loose stones, and then sat for a long time looking out over the herd. He said nothing to the others when he eventually joined them for the evening meal, but his eyes were cold and glittering with anger. Ootek too was downcast, sad at the loss of the dog and somehow feeling guilty, as if he had in part been responsible for the death.

A few days later Anak attacked Carver, and only the timely intervention of Handsome saved him from serious injury or worse. When he was not acting as leader of the dog team Handsome usually stayed close to Carver, accompanying him on his frequent hunting trips. On this occasion Carver was returning to camp, skirting the side of the hill and cutting across a corner of the meadow.

The reindeer herd grazed close by, but Carver paid them little heed, until he heard a sudden low grunting and looked up to see Anak charging towards him. Even then Carver felt little premonition of danger, certain that the bull would stop short of pressing home his attack. Too late he realized he was mistaken and turned to run. There was no cover within five hundred yards, and Carver was hampered by the tussocks of grass and the soft squelchy ground that dragged at his feet with every step. Belatedly he thought to unsling the rifle he carried over his shoulder. There was no time to take aim, and he was about to use the weapon as a club when Handsome raced in to attack, narrowly escaping being brained in the process.

He sprang at Anak's throat, his teeth clashing together in the thick white mane of hair, but without penetrating to the skin. As his grip failed Handsome dropped to the ground in front of the bull, and the two circled warily as Carver worked a round into the breech of his rifle and thumbed over the safety catch.

It was a classic stand-off situation. Handsome was unable to see an opening beyond the spreading antlers of the bull. Anak had no intention of exposing his flanks. Carver dared not fire for fear of hitting the dog. As quickly as it had risen, Anak's temper cooled, and slowly he began to back off, one step at a time, his head still lowered as a shield against attack. With each movement Handsome followed him until at last, uncertain whether or not to continue, he glanced back at Carver. Anak chose that moment to turn and bolt, back to the safety of the herd.

'You should have shot him,' Abner said later that night. 'I'd sooner wear his hide on my back than the scars from those antlers. He is evil, that one.'

'Aw, come on,' pleaded Carver. 'He's just feisty with the rut. He's feeling his oats, is all.'

'He is a good bull,' said Ootek. 'See how big and strong he is. He will father many fine calves.'

'Big calves, you mean,' said Abner. 'Big calves mean trouble at birth. I think it better he goes, soon, before he causes any more trouble. We have two other bulls to journey north with us, so we can spare him.'

'You had three before, remember?' asked Carver. 'And what happened? You lost the lot.'

Grumbling, Abner subsided, and Carver abruptly changed the subject.

'Winter's fast approaching,' he announced. 'Isn't it time we moved on? The grazing here is almost all used up.'

Reluctantly, for he'd almost grown used to living in one place, Abner had to agree. It hardly seemed possible that the deer could strip an entire valley bare of vegetation, yet whole areas had been denuded of their covering of moss. Grasses and plants had been uprooted and left to wither and die. The ground was pitted with hoof prints, and the new tender shoots of willow and birch had been bitten back to older wood. The deer were greedy and rapacious feeders, and they wasted as much as they ate.

At length it was decided that they should move as soon as the first snows covered the ground. Now a sense of urgency gripped all three as they began to make preparations to leave the valley. Carver shot another moose, a young bull, and they spent the rest of the day cutting the meat into thin strips and drying it over smoke. Thus preserved it would be light to carry and would keep indefinitely. It could be used as a nourishing basis for soups and stews, and the strips could be chewed to sustain their strength on the trail.

Carver checked the lashings on his sledge and made a thorough inspection of all the dogs' harnesses, renewing any parts that were roughened or worn. A dog that was not comfortable in its harness would not pull willingly, and if forced would quickly develop sores where the harness chafed and thus become a burden to the whole team.

All three men were in need of new boots and gloves, and Abner spent a week curing and tanning the hide of the moose Carver had shot. First he soaked the hide in water to which he had added a mixture of wood ash and fat. Next he scraped away the hair and any particles of flesh or fat still adhering, before smearing it with grease and smoking it over a slow fire. Then he immersed it once more in a solution of ash and fat, to which he had added the rotten brains of the moose. Many hours of work followed, stretching, rubbing, scraping and wringing, before the final smoking transformed the stinking hide into a thing of beauty, supple, golden and fragrant.

Meanwhile Ootek, grumbling all the while that it was woman's work, renewed the rawhide webbing on three pairs of snowshoes. Secretly he had hoped to ride the big bull on the trail ahead, but the rut was now under way, and though he still tolerated the boy's presence Anak had made it quite plain that he was preoccupied with other matters. Regretfully, Ootek decided it would be better to walk.

Each day the battle for the supremacy of the herd was fought anew. The smallest of the three bulls retired early, after being severely punished by the other two, and thereafter remained apart from the herd, loitering morosely in a far corner of the valley. The other, though smaller and lighter than Anak, seemed possessed of an inexhaustible energy. Each time Anak chased him away from one group of cows, he would circle round and rejoin the herd at the opposite end.

As time passed the smaller bull became bolder, more self-confident, lingering just a little longer before taking

56

flight. Now Anak grew cunning, stalking his prey rather than charging him, sneaking quietly towards him and dropping his head as though to feed whenever the smaller bull showed signs of nervousness. Twice Anak almost succeeded, but each time his victim escaped.

Early one morning, as a thick mist blanketed the valley in a chill, moisture-laden shroud and the men were still sound asleep, Anak attacked again. This time, as his quarry turned to flee, Anak's antlers caught him low on the flank, throwing him off balance and sending him sprawling on the ground. As the bull struggled to regain his feet Anak charged him head on and their antlers locked in a jarring crash. For the space of a few yards Anak drove him back, gathering speed and momentum as his superior weight and strength overpowered those of the smaller bull. As his opponent collapsed Anak thrust hard once more, driving the bull's head between his forelegs, dislocating his neck just below the point where it entered his skull. It was all over. Anak shook himself free and trotted away, leaving the corpse of his rival lying still on the ground.

To the others' secret surprise, Abner said nothing on seeing the dead bull. Later however, when Carver and Ootek returned from butchering the carcase they found him sitting grimly at work, filing a series of notches along the back of his hunting knife. Ootek was horrified when he heard Abner's plan, and he refused to have anything to do with the operation.

'Cutting off his antlers would be like scalping my brother,' he exclaimed, and sat brooding by the fire as the others went off to catch Anak.

It was easy enough to rope Anak, but wrestling him down so that they could tie his legs and immobilize him was another matter. Anak had grown in strength and stature during the few months that had passed since they first caught him and they had to put two lassoes over his head before they could even get near him. Even then they were thrown about like rag dolls before they could get hold of his antlers and throw him off balance. Once he was down Anak lay still, and though bruised and breathing hard, Abner was able to go to work with his primitive saw.

The amputation caused Anak no pain, for the blood and nerve supply to his antlers had long since withered and died, but it took a while to saw through the bone-hard growth, and the shock to his system was great. After it was over they removed the ties and jumped clear, but Anak lay still, exhausted by his struggles and breathing in great shuddering gasps. After a few minutes he scrambled unsteadily to his feet, shaking his head in bewilderment at what had befallen him, but it was late in the day before he started grazing again. Throughout that time he had showed no interest in the harem he had fought to gain, but to Ootek's relief he seemed back to normal by the following day, and the loss of his antlers seemed to cause no impairment to his vigour.

Yet although the experience had shaken his faith in humans, Anak still trusted Ootek. In refusing to take any part in the task of removing the bull's antlers, Ootek had recoiled instinctively, but by so doing he had kept intact the bond that existed between him and the deer. So although Anak now avoided both Abner and Carver, he still allowed Ootek to approach him as before.

Three days later the wind changed and began to blow from the west. Clouds massed in dark array, veiling the peaks of the mountains, and towards evening the first snow flakes fell. By morning the storm had passed, but the world lay glistening white, and ice rimed the fringes of the stream.

The men were astir early, folding the hide coverings of their tents and loading the sledge first. Abner had to catch up and harness the two cows he used as pack animals, so it was nearing noon by the time they were ready to depart. One of the cows was a barren one, the natural herd leader, and Abner knew that wherever she went the others would follow. Secretly Abner had felt some doubts as to whether the wild caribou bulls would follow the herd, since their natural inclination was to drift south at this time of year. He need not have worried. The instinct to stay with the herd overcame all other desires. The bulls followed the cows, Anak as usual somewhere in the middle of the herd, the other trotting irresolutely in the rear. Ootek alternated between helping Abner lead, and ranging along the sides of the herd. Carver came last.

He discovered that there were advantages to dog sledding behind a reindeer herd, for the deer broke a wide trail of hard-packed snow over which the sled runners ran easily, and on level or downward-sloping ground he could even ride for long distances. Mostly though he preferred to walk, because the light breeze had a bite to it which made sedentary travel uncomfortable.

They headed north and east. Carver just hoped Abner knew where he was going. Though the coastline, from Sitka to Point Barrow, had long been surveyed, most of the interior lay unmapped, the rivers unnamed, the mountains uncharted. Carver had some knowledge of the lie of the land. He knew that the mighty Yukon lay to the south, and that to the west the vast empty space of the Seward peninsula jutted far out into the sea. Of the lands that lay between them and the north coast, and the people who might or might not inhabit them, he had only the sketchiest of knowledge, gleaned from some half-forgotten yarns beside a camp fire or a bar and adding mystery to their venture.

The deer set their own pace, seemingly eager to be on the move soon after the sun rose above the horizon, but after ten or fifteen miles beginning to slow down, and to stop and graze. As the days merged one with the other in the way of great journeys, the treeless hills gave way to moist tundra carpeted with a shrubby growth of willow, alder,

59

resinous birch and Labrador tea. Apart from the deer and themselves, and the ubiquitous scavenging ravens, the wilderness seemed almost devoid of life. Occasionally an eagle would glide in great lazy circles overhead. Once they sighted a herd of mountain sheep grazing on a distant hill, and once a solitary wolf exploring a gravel bar. Of human habitation there was no sign.

The days grew shorter and the nights colder, and more snow fell. Yet Carver never failed to be astonished at the ease with which the deer found forage, digging down through the snow with their forehooves and laying bare the lichen and dried grass on which they subsisted. Deer were easier to keep than dogs, he decided. As he had feared, game had proved scarce for some time now, and their supplies of moose and caribou meat were running low. So far the long leisure hours at the end of each day had provided ample time for hunting, but he had enjoyed little success, except for one memorable evening when he had shot two sheep. The rich, greasy mutton had made a pleasant change, and yielded a welcome supply of fat as well as releasing some of the dried moose meat for the dogs, but now they were on short rations, and he was thankful that he did not have to work them too hard.

Afterwards Carver could never remember whether it was towards the end of the eleventh or the thirteenth day that they came to the river. It flowed swift and strong towards the west, forming a massive oxbow in the valley among the hills. Within the curve of the bow lay a wide hummocky plain, and aspen and balsam poplar and thick forests of spruce cloaked the sides of the hills around.

They stood gazing across at the far bank with some awe. The river was the greatest obstacle they had come across so far, for though ice rimed the shores and coated the eddies the main stream had yet to freeze over; unless they could find a shallower stretch, crossing would be an ordeal for both men and beasts. It was, they decided, a problem that could wait until the morning. The deer had spread out and were grazing quietly, and Carver was just sweeping a space clear of snow prior to making camp for the night when a shout from Ootek drew his attention. Looking downriver, in the direction Ootek was pointing, Carver saw a thin column of smoke rising above the trees.

5

The Siwash Girl

'Siwash,' said Abner.

Carver didn't think so. Indians, in his experience, lit small fires of dry sticks which burned with a clear flame, unless they were smoking fish or meat. Then they took pains to see that the smoke was dispersed among the trees. They did not believe in betraying their whereabouts in so obvious a manner.

He thought for a moment. 'I'll sneak over and take a look. I don't suppose there'll be any trouble, but it's best not to advertise our presence until we're sure. Look, if there's any real danger, I'll fire one shot. That's maybe all I'll get time for. If you hear it, gather the herd and move upriver. I'll catch up when I can.'

He stepped into his snowshoes, shouldered his rifle and unhitched Handsome from where he lay tethered. Then he set off downriver, the dog following silently at his heel. The air was very still. Though the light still lingered the temperature was falling rapidly as the frost began to bite. A grey jay burst from a spruce tree with a whirr of wings and a high-pitched, scraping cry, startling both him and the dog. As he drew nearer to the source of the smoke he stopped often to listen, straining his ears for he knew not what – the sound of an axe, the cries of children, the sudden warning bark of a dog.

There was nothing, only the soft whisper of his snowshoes and the gentle rasp of his breath. The camp, who ever it belonged to, lay by the river, beyond a thick stand of willow, now leafless and bare. Peering through the network of twigs he could see the fire, thick logs smouldering slow, and beside it the seated figure of a man, his back turned towards him. Even from that distance Carver could see he was a giant of a man, tall and thickset, with a breadth of shoulder that, even allowing for the thick clothing, was remarkable. Carver unslung his rifle, slipped off the safety catch and cradled the weapon in the crook of his arm in the manner of a hunter. He didn't want to cause unnecessary offence, but he figured it was better to be in rude health than dead, and some people took an instant dislike to strangers appearing suddenly out of the bush.

'Hi there,' he called.

There was no response. Carver tried again. 'Hullo, stranger. Mind if I join you?'

Still there was no reply. The figure neither moved nor turned his head. He just sat, as if turned to stone, and Carver felt the hair begin to prickle at the back of his head. Slowly he moved forward, a step at a time, until he stood beside the seated figure.

The man sat staring out across the river, one leg stretched stiffly in front of him, his boot almost in the fire, the other leg drawn protectively up to his chest. In his hand he held a folded scrap of paper. He looked like a man who had just been the recipient of bad news, which was true in a way, for he was dead.

He could not have been dead long, no more than an hour or so at most. A dixie set on the fire had boiled dry. As far as Carver could see, it had contained nothing but water. Gingerly he reached down and plucked the paper from the cold fingers. With the careful deliberation of one long unused to such an exercise, Carver spelled out the message:

My leg is broke, and I'm like to die. Whoever finds me can keep my goods and wepons, in return for a Christian burial. Signed: Aaron Coates.

63

*

It was not unusual for a lone traveller to make a last will and testament. Carver had heard of many such cases in the past. It was the codicil that excited him more. Added lower down the page, in barely decipherable print, it spelled:

> Give the gold to the Siwash girl. She knowed me. AC.

There was a pick and shovel, and a gold pan, standard equipment of the miner. There was a good knife, a twelve-gauge shotgun, a Remington repeater rifle, and two Colt .45 revolvers with seven-inch barrels. The man was a walking arsenal, thought Carver. There was a plentiful supply of ammunition, there was tea, salt, sugar, and best of all tobacco, but not a scrap of food. Even so, it made a considerable load, causing Carver to wonder what fear, real or imaginary, had made the man overburden himself with firearms in this way.

All the while, as he made an inventory of his sudden inheritance, Carver pondered the riddle of the miner's death. He must have been on his way back from his claim, wherever that was, to where? Civilization perhaps, wherever *that* was, and his Siwash girl, whoever she was? And where was the gold?

He found it, about two ounces of it, in a pouch strapped to the man's waist under several layers of heavy serge clothing and flannel underwear. In a side pocket of the man's coat he also found a bible, the fly leaf missing, which explained the piece of paper in his hand.

In the end he left everything where he had found it, except the gold and the will, and went back to find Abner and Ootek. On the way he had a short tussle with his conscience, and by the time he reached the camp he had decided to show Abner the will. Since Ootek could not read, and in any case knew nothing about gold or its value, he didn't count.

They used the miner's tools to dig a shallow grave in the gravel, and together they managed to lay him to rest. Abner had been tempted to examine the broken leg, but the stench of putrefaction soon made him desist. It was the sort of accident that could easily happen. A sudden slip on a loose stone or ice, and the damage was done, especially if the man had been carrying a heavy load. Then, alone in the wilderness, without help of any kind to hand, he was doomed.

As a last gesture Carver placed the bible beneath the miner's crossed arms, and then they filled in the grave, covering it with rocks to prevent the wolves and bears from digging up the corpse. They left his pick and shovel as a headstone and took the rest of his gear back to camp. Carver kept the Colts, and Abner the Remington. The shotgun they gave to Ootek.

Later that evening, after they had eaten and were sitting round the fire, Carver produced the will.

Abner studied it in silence for a while. 'What do you make of it all?' he queried.

'Way I see it,' said Carver, 'he spent the summer prospecting, somewhere up the river. He set off back to a settlement to pass the winter, maybe with his Siwash girl, carrying just enough food to last his journey. He broke his leg, couldn't get along, ate all his rations, and died of starvation and blood poisoning. Happens all the time, especially to a man travelling alone.'

'Why the armoury though?' persisted Abner. 'Looked to me like a man expecting trouble, lots of it.'

'Maybe they weren't all his. Maybe he had a partner once.'

'Dead?'

'Have to be,' said Carver. 'You wouldn't leave a man alone without arms in this country.'

Abner thought for a moment. 'Unless they fell out. Unless Coates was afraid this partner would follow him, take him by surprise one night.'

'Bushwhack him, you mean,' said Carver. 'That's a sight too much thinking for a man to go to bed on. We've no proof of any of this.'

'Maybe they fell out over the gold.'

'All two ounces,' scoffed Carver. 'Why, it's hardly enough to buy a man a decent grubstake.'

Fleetingly it crossed Abner's mind that Carver could be lying about the gold. Then he dismissed the idea. Carver need not have mentioned it at all, need not have shown him the will. He fell to studying it again.

'Give the gold to the Siwash girl. She knowed me.' He paused, pondering a moment. 'I wonder if he meant that in the bible way?'

'How do you mean, "bible way" '? asked Carver.

'You know, in Genesis: "And Cain knew his wife; and she conceived.".'

Carver looked at him admiringly. 'You know, you should have been a storyteller. You've got more mystery out of that bit o' paper than I'd 've believed possible.'

He yawned and stretched, then kicked the fire together and watched the flames leap higher. 'I dunno though. Only one reason why he should know an Indian girl, and so it's very likely she is pregnant. Like breaking a leg, it happens all the time. Only sleeping with a Siwash girl is a lot more fun.'

'You speak of her as if she were no more than a dog,' said Ootek suddenly.

Both men started. They had been so engrossed in Aaron Coates's will that they had forgotten about Ootek sitting silently beside them. From not being able to understand a word of English, Ootek during the past few months had learned to speak a considerable amount. As it happened, he understood English better than he could speak it, much

66

more than Abner or Carver realized. So, though he was unable to read, he was well able to understand the gist of the conversation that had just passed. He also knew about gold, and the greed white men had for the soft yellow metal. It had always been a source of constant wonder to his people. Suddenly he felt a flare of anger at the way he was being excluded from the discussion, mingled with disgust at the casual manner in which they talked about 'the Siwash girl'.

'You people come to this land,' he went on. 'You take our friendship, our food, our furs. You share our homes, and even our wives. You take everything you want, and give us nothing but disease and starvation in return.'

'Hey now! What's got into you all of a sudden?' demanded Carver. 'Far as I can recall, there was never any love lost between your people and the Siwash. There was always more fighting than trading between you. Why are you so keen to defend them all of a sudden? And what's all this about taking and not giving? Seems to me we've given you a better deal than you had before we came along. You can always go back to your Nunamiut friends if you don't like our company.'

'You asked me to come along,' replied Ootek hotly. 'You asked for my help. Remember?'

'Now, now, now,' said Abner soothingly. 'No one's going back anywhere. What is it about women and gold anyhow? Here we were travelling together as quietly and as peacefully as you please. Then all of a sudden there's talk of women and gold, and we're fighting like a nest of bobcats.'

'I'm not fighting,' said Carver. 'I'm stating facts, is all.'

'So what are you going to do about it?' demanded Ootek.

'About what?' asked Carver.

'About the girl, and the gold?'

'Do?' asked Carver wonderingly. 'Nothing, is what we do. Even supposing we knew where to look for this Siwash girl, how do we know when we've found her? We don't know her name, or what she looks like.' He paused, reflecting on his own past a moment. 'He could have known several Siwash girls.'

'I think maybe he knew *this* one,' said Ootek.

The girl stood on the edge of the clearing, her outline clearly visible in the flames of the fire Carver had just kicked together. Even her thick cladding of furs failed to hide the swelling beneath her robe. She had the high cheekbones of the Koyukon Indian, and a dark, wild beauty that was enhanced by a look of fierce stubborn pride – like a falcon, Ootek thought. Then, as she stepped nearer the fire he saw that her beauty was marred by a pronounced limp. Her left leg was shortened and bowed, her whole body twisted to one side as if to compensate for the infirmity. In one hand she carried a brace of ptarmigan, their white plumage glowing in the dark. She dropped the birds at Carver's feet, and then quite suddenly fell down beside them, collapsing as if she had been shot.

She managed to drink some soup and eat a little of the meat left over from the evening meal, but before she could manage more than a mouthful she was asleep. They made up the fire and left her beside it on a couch of skins. Next morning when they awoke she was sitting up and plucking the two ptarmigan she had brought with her the night before. As she worked, she told them her story.

Her name, she said, was Kyloo, which means Willow. Her injuries had been caused by an accident in her early childhood, when she had fallen in a fire. Everyone had thought she would die, but an old fur trader had found her and nursed her back to life. In return she had stayed with the white man, looking after him until he died, and then she had set out to find her own people again. On the way she had met Aaron Coates, and she had spent the summer with him, prospecting for gold in the headwaters of the river. They had found little, and were on their way

68

downriver, heading for the coast, when Aaron had slipped and broken his leg.

'How come you were so short of food?' asked Carver.

'We did not go short,' replied Kyloo, a hint of pride in her voice. 'I caught fish, trapped birds, snared rabbits. But Aaron could not eat. He had sickness, fever, sometimes he shivered and talked wild. I think it was the poison in his leg.'

She laid the plucked carcase of the ptarmigan in the snow, and brushed the feathers from her lap. 'I was returning with these, hoping to make him some soup, when I saw you. Then I was afraid, and so I hid.'

Carver nodded. It made sense. Then, 'Why all the guns?'

A scowl of anger crossed the girl's face. 'Many bad men hereabouts. White men rob Indians, steal their wives. Indians kill white men, take their knives, guns. Sometimes white men rob each other. This is a dangerous place.'

Carver sat silent a moment, digesting this. 'What made you think you could trust us?'

Kyloo shrugged, and gestured to Abner and Ootek. 'White man and Inupiat friends. Besides, I watched you bury Aaron, and put the holy book in his arms before you covered the grave. Bad men do not do these things.'

She hadn't asked about the gold, although she must have known of its existence. Maybe she thought it was buried with Aaron. Yet Carver was acutely aware that Ootek was watching him, and he guessed what was on the boy's mind. He pulled out the pouch and tossed it over to Kyloo.

'Aaron left you that,' he said gruffly.

To his intense surprise the girl started back, recoiling from the gold as if from a striking snake. Then she picked up a short stick and pushed the pouch back towards him, refusing to touch it with her hand.

'I do not want it,' she hissed. 'It makes men bad.'

Suddenly she seemed to change her mind. Leaning forward she grabbed the pouch, her fingers clawing at the string drawn tightly round its neck. Next moment, before anyone could move to stop her she swung the open pouch in a wide, sweeping arc.

The dust flew out in a shimmering haze, high in the clear morning air. Then slowly it drifted to earth, settling on the hair, shoulders and faces of the men who sat around. The empty pouch fell into the fire, where it dissolved in a small cloud of acrid smoke. Carver gazed at the girl blankly for a while, then he looked at the gilded faces of his companions, and he started to laugh.

One by one the others joined in, until even the girl began to smile. Then suddenly Carver was serious again.

'Best we don't hang around these parts too long, if what we've heard is true.' He turned to Kyloo. 'Guess you'll be heading back to join your own folks now?'

Kyloo shook her head. 'How would I know where to find them?' she queried.

Carver shrugged. 'You can't come with us,' he announced flatly.

The girl said nothing. She just sat, head bowed, staring into the fire, and she seemed to shrink into the folds of her parka as if to pretend she were not there at all. The others began to fold their tents and load up the sledge. Carver endured the silence for a while and then gave vent to his exasperation.

'It's out of the question,' he exclaimed. 'She's crippled, for God's sake!'

'She walked here,' observed Ootek sullenly.

'And she's pregnant.'

Abner grinned. 'She won't be for long, by the look of her.'

Carver kicked savagely at a bundle of hides. 'We're trying to run a reindeer herd here, not start a goddamned village. Look! Coates's will said: "Give the gold to the

70

Siwash girl.". We did that. It didn't say: "Take the Siwash with you and train her to be a reindeer herder.". Did it?'

'I want the girl to come along with us,' said Ootek.

Carver looked at him appraisingly for a while, and then he grinned. 'We know exactly what you want, son. I don't blame you. Felt the same way myself once. Now if you want to enjoy this young lady, you stay right here, cause there's no room for home comforts along the trail. Or you . . .'

He never finished what he had to say. Ootek came at him in a crouching spring, and next moment he would have had Carver by the throat were it not for Handsome, who seized him by the arm and flung him to the ground. Luckily Ootek's thick parka sleeve saved him from being badly bitten, but even so the power of Handsome's jaws threatened to crush his arm.

At a word from Carver Handsome released his hold, and Carver stood staring down at Ootek, who glowered back at him from the snow.

'You coming north, or what?' Carver demanded. 'Make up your mind.'

Ootek scrambled miserably to his feet and dusted the snow from his pants. He was trapped, and he knew it. If he stayed with the girl everyone would believe it was for only one reason, even though she was pregnant. He could not allow them to think that, especially since he half knew it to be true. In any case he could not sacrifice his plans to go north, to find the land where he was born, especially since after the baby's birth, the girl might well forsake him for one of the others.

The girl was still sitting there when they mustered the herd and started to move off upriver. She had neither moved nor spoken. Every once in a while Ootek paused to look back, hoping for he knew not what, perhaps to see her following, or perhaps heading in another direction. Each time he stopped she was still in the same position, her dark figure dwindling in the distance. The same anger

71

and frustration he had experienced the night before seethed within him. Only now it was not he who was being excluded, but the girl. The thought came to him unbidden: When they want us, they use us.

When next he looked round the figure of the girl had vanished behind a fold in the ground. Abruptly, he turned about and set off back. Carver watched him go.

'Well,' he said to himself, 'I guess that's the last we've seen of him.'

He had been so confident that Ootek would not return that he was surprised, a short time later, to see the young Eskimo hurrying back towards them. He was alone, and briefly, Carver wondered what had happened to the girl. He did not have to wait long to find out.

'Kyloo tells me that there is no way across the river this way,' Ootek announced. 'The water is deep for many miles upstream. Downriver, the crossing is easy.'

Carver swore viciously. They should have checked for a crossing before they set out. Now the Siwash girl had made fools of them all. Next thing they knew, she'd be in charge of the outfit. Abner was more philosophical. Cheerfully he set about the tedious business of turning back the herd, the deer grunting and protesting as they jostled into their rightful positions. Then they set off back the way they had come, Carver morosely bringing up the rear.

6

Kyloo's Baby

By the end of the third day it became obvious that Carver had been right, and that Kyloo had neither the speed nor the stamina to keep up with the march. Each morning she started well enough, but after a few hours she began to lag further and further behind, eventually limping into camp an hour or more after the others had arrived, too exhausted and weary to do more than collapse beside the fire.

Each evening Carver waited for her to beg to ride on the sledge. He was determined not to make the offer first. Though she had saved them many weary miles of travel, the humiliation he had felt still rankled, especially since the crossing she had shown them was so shallow that the water barely came over their knees.

Maybe Kyloo sensed this. Maybe it was just pride that forbade her to ask the favour; maybe it was fear of refusal. Or maybe the thought simply hadn't occurred to her. For centuries generations of women had walked the length and breadth of the land, load carriers like the dogs, following their men, the hunters. Women had given birth on the trail, stepping aside and seeking the shelter of a few bushes. Kneeling in the snow they had delivered themselves of their offspring, and walked on, but they hadn't been crippled.

Towards the end of the third day they made camp at the mouth of a ravine high in the mountains. It was a poor sort of place for the deer. A shallow stream flowed through the centre, but all around the land was stony and barren. Each winter the wind howled and shrieked through this gash in the hills, whipping away the protective covering of snow. Each spring the melt water from the snow turned the stream into a raging torrent, tearing away the thin covering of topsoil. So little vegetation grew, but there was a thin belt of trees higher on the hill, which gave shelter from the wind and kindling for their fire.

Abner was fretful and impatient for once. The worst months of the winter were fast approaching, and he was anxious to get down out of the high hills and find warmer, more sheltered lands, where the moss grew thick and the trees stood tall. He felt uneasy in this alien land, with its ever present threat of danger.

Ootek sat brooding by the fire, watching and waiting for Kyloo to come limping along the trail. Over the past few days he had grown more and more alienated from the other two men. Abner did not seem to care whether the girl lived or died. Carver had made it plain from the start that he did not want her along. Only he, Ootek, seemed to have any concern for her welfare. It was not, as Carver supposed, mere lust on his part, though he had to admit that nightly the image of her face and the ripe curves of her body haunted his dreams and disturbed his sleep. Nor was it pity, he told himself. Rather, he felt a common bond with her, for they were both alone in the world, he an orphan, and she rejected by her parents.

Several times in the past few days he had wondered if she could ride Anak. He was sure he could persuade the bull to let her mount him, but his temper was still uncertain after the rut, and while Ootek himself could cheerfully survive a tumble into the snow, he was not sure what harm it would do to a pregnant woman. It was a chance, he decided, he could not afford to take.

The men had finished their meal and were sitting back relaxing and estimating the many miles still to come, smoking and drinking tea. The deer had sought the shelter of the trees and were out of sight of the camp. Dusk was falling, but there was still no sign of Kyloo. Ootek quietly got up from the fire and set off towards the trees, taking with him a length of rawhide.

The deer knew him now and, recognizing him by sight and smell, showed no sign of fear. He found Anak browsing contentedly on a thicket of willow. The bull welcomed him by blowing softly down his nostrils, and Ootek stood fondling him for a while, then slipped the bridle he had fashioned out of the rawhide over Anak's head.

At first Anak was reluctant to leave his willow bush, but after a little gentle coaxing he allowed himself to be led away. Ootek trotted swiftly through the trees, circling round the back of the camp and dropping downhill away from the ravine without the others noticing he was gone.

Once clear of the camp he halted Anak and stood for a moment, mustering his courage. Then, scarce daring to breathe, he sank his fingers deep into Anak's mane, and when he had a secure hold on the thick guard hairs he eased himself gently on to the bull's back.

Anak started at first, and took a few nervous sideways steps, but Ootek's soft voice calmed him. Then the persistent prodding of Ootek's heels drove him forward. Soon, to Ootek's joy, he was trotting, swinging into the long easy stride that was faster than a man could run, a tireless pace that could, if need be, carry him sixty miles in a day.

Ootek's style of riding was strictly unorthodox. He lay rather than sat on the bull. Though he retained hold of the reins his hands were fully occupied hanging on to the thick cape of hair that protected Anak's shoulders. His body and chest were pressed tight to the bull's back, while his knees and heels gripped the flanks.

Darkness was falling fast now, and the wind moaned eerily across the land, gusting down from the peaks and whipping whirls of snow across the frozen wastes. The howling of the wind made Ootek think of wolves, and he cursed himself for not bringing his shotgun. He clung on tight and buried his face in Anak's cape, feeling the warmth

75

of the bull's body beneath him, while an icy wind chilled his back.

The moon rose, leaping up from behind the hills as though fired from a gun. Clouds, driven by the wind, raced across its face, so that the flickering light waxed and waned, one moment bathing the landscape in brilliant light, and the next plunging it into deep shadow.

He nearly missed her, an inert bundle half lying beside the trail. It was Anak who alerted him, snorting with terror and leaping sideways, so that he almost threw his rider in the snow. Ootek dismounted, and keeping firm hold on the bridle, led the trembling animal to where she lay. Then it was her turn to cry out in terror, as she woke to find a caribou bull near to stamping on her.

Almost sobbing with relief and frustration Ootek calmed the nervous bull and asked Kyloo if she could stand. After an interval the girl struggled to her feet and stood swaying with exhaustion and cold.

'You ride,' he told her. 'You'll be quite safe. Here, hold on to his hair. Make friends with him.'

Had she not been so weary, had she not been half conscious from cold, exhaustion and lack of food, she might not have summoned up the courage to make the attempt. Perhaps because she was a woman, and her sex posed no threat, Anak suffered her attentions with no more than a nervous snort of fear. Then he stood quietly as Ootek assisted her to mount.

The journey back to camp took longer. Ootek dared not urge Anak into a trot, for fear the girl would be thrown. As it was, with every step he expected her to fall asleep and slide off into the snow. 'You awake?' he kept demanding, and only when he heard her answer would he desist.

As the wind grew stronger and the night colder, the heat from Anak's body kept Kyloo warm, but Ootek, walking slowly in front, was exposed to the full fury of the gale. Frozen snow whipped up by the wind stung his face,

76

freezing and blinding him. From time to time he slipped his hand from his mitt and massaged his frozen cheeks, aware of the numbness that warned of impending frostbite. All his teaching told him they should stop and hole up in the snow, but he did not think Kyloo could survive the night. He too was feeling fatigue at the end of yet another long day. Now he marvelled at the distance he had travelled in that short exhilarating ride down the trail.

At last, stumbling with fatigue and half blinded by the snow, he saw the welcome glow of the camp fire. Now Anak would approach no nearer, so Ootek put his arm around Kyloo and helped her to slide from the bull's back before turning him loose to rejoin the herd. Then he led her to the fire.

The others were nowhere to be seen, but the sound of snoring issuing from their tents spoke of their lack of concern. Still, there was soup left heating by the fire, and this was enough to warm and comfort them. Afterwards, Kyloo started to make up her bed as usual beside the fire, but Ootek led her instead to his tent. He was about to leave her there when she caught his hand.

He stood there hesitant, unsure of what she wanted of him, not knowing what to do or say. She knelt down on the couch of skins, drawing him down beside her, and his heart began to beat faster as she slipped out of her robes. After a moment he did the same, and together they nestled down among the furs. Then, folding him in her arms, Kyloo clasped his head to her breast and fell sound asleep.

Ootek lay awake for a long time, acutely aware of the satin smoothness of her skin and the soft rounded curves of the body pressed close to his own. A low moan escaped him as the intensity of his desire for her grew, but he made no move to disturb her. Instead he lay still, listening to the sound of her soft breathing. Gradually a deep inner peace stole over him and he was content just to lie in the comfort of her arms, her full breast for a pillow, and the gossamer feel of her hair caressing his cheek.

In the end he must have fallen asleep, for towards dawn he woke with a start, aware of a change in Kyloo's breathing. Now it was harsh and loud, coming in great gasps, and from time to time she moaned. He reached over and gripped her by the arms, and in the light of the setting moon he saw her eyes, dark and glittering with fear and her white teeth bared in a grimace of pain.

'Baby!' she grunted. 'Baby come.'

Now he knew only terror and rushed from her side, flinging himself down by the fire and holding his head in his hands, covering his ears to shut out the sound of her screams. But the cries continued, until at last Abner emerged from his tent, rubbing the sleep from his eyes and peering round.

Ootek waved towards his tent. 'Baby come,' he shouted, and covered his ears again.

Abner nodded casually and sauntered over to the tent. After a brief glance inside he lifted the flap and entered. He was gone a long time, but the cries gradually lessened and soon all was still. The pre-dawn light had lengthened into day before he emerged, carrying something purple and black which he buried under the snow. Then he washed his hands, and sheathing the short knife he had used to cut the cord he walked over to the fire and slapped Ootek on the back, just as if he were the father.

'Big baby,' he announced. 'A fine boy.'

'They all right?' asked Ootek.

Abner nodded. 'Came quickly in the end, just like reindeer calf, only easier. The cord was round his neck, but that was no problem.'

Ootek smiled, only half comprehending, but he felt a wave of relief and happiness.

Even Carver seemed pleased, though he was inclined to make light of the matter. 'Siwash women never have any trouble. Whelp like bitches, most of 'em.'

Later, his courage quite restored, Ootek peeped in on Kyloo as she lay on the couch of skins, cradling the baby in her arms. Only his eyes betrayed his mixed parentage. With them closed, the infant looked just like another Indian, with olive skin and a shock of jet-black hair. When he opened them, they shone a piercing blue.

Kyloo looked shyly up at him. 'See my baby bull!' she murmured.

Ootek stretched out one finger to touch the baby's brow. 'Abner says he came as easy as a reindeer calf,' he said

'How do you say "caribou" in your tongue? asked Kyloo.

'Tuktu,' replied Ootek.

Kyloo held the baby out at arm's length and gazed at him. 'Then that shall be his name,' she announced, 'for it was a caribou bull that saved him, and his mother, from freezing in the snow.'

She smiled, and turning to Ootek she laid her hand on his arm. 'And you,' she whispered. 'Thank you. It was brave, coming back to find me.'

Embarrassed, Ootek fled to find some breakfast.

Already the others were packing up, ready to move out and continue the journey. The deer were hungry and restless, and Abner knew that at any time they would move of their own accord in search of fresh grazing, and he would be powerless to stop them. Ootek sat on alone by the fire, taking no part in the activity. He was deeply grateful to Abner, and thankful for his skill and kindness in delivering the baby, but he could not forgive Carver's callous and indifferent attitude to the plight of the Indian girl.

Though part of him wanted to move on with the herd and seek a new life in the north, he knew that if they all four stayed together it would increase the existing tension. In any case, Kyloo had not been able to keep up with them even before the birth. Now, if anything, she was weaker, and he did not think she could ride the caribou so soon after her confinement. Even if Carver relented sufficiently to let her ride on the sledge it would not be practical. He remembered the journey they had made transporting the three bulls, and the battering and shaking they had received. He did not think Kyloo could endure such a jolting for long.

After some thought he went over to Abner, who was harnessing one of the deer he used as pack animals. 'I've decided it would be best if we stay here,' he announced, 'Kyloo and me.'

Abner nodded in agreement. Secretly he felt relieved that they would not be burdened with the girl, but unlike Carver, who seemed to have no compunction about the matter, he had felt troubled at the way Kyloo had been treated.

'Also, I would like to keep the caribou bull,' went on Ootek.

Abner thought about this for a moment. He knew nothing about the part the bull had played in the rescue the night before, and had merely assumed that Ootek had gone in search of Kyloo on foot. Yet he knew of the affinity that existed between the boy and the big bull.

In a way he regretted losing Ootek more than the bull. He had grown fond of the boy and would miss his company. The big bull had served its purpose as sire to the herd. Other than that, it had been nothing but trouble. He had another bull, and several promising youngsters coming along. Ootek was entitled to some reward for his assistance during the past months, and this was perhaps as good a way of repaying him as any. At least it would cost nothing.

'Keep the bull,' Abner said shortly. Then another thought struck him. 'When we move off he's going to try to follow the herd, and you are going to have a fight on your hands if you try to stop him. Go now, and hobble his front legs. Tie him to a tree by the antlers, and cover his eyes with a piece of hide so he cannot watch the others leave. Wait until we are long gone before you release him, and leave the hobbles on. Otherwise he will still follow.'

Later Ootek was to feel even more grateful to Abner. As the herd moved away out of the ravine, Anak plunged and fought, straining against the ties that bound him. His efforts were in vain. The plaited rawhide held fast, despite his strength, and as the sounds of the departing herd died away his struggles ceased and he stood quiet and trembling.

As he was about to leave, Carver grinned across at Ootek, still sitting beside the fire. 'So you got yourself a readymade family then, son? Well, I wish you luck. You'll need it.' Chuckling to himself, he whipped up his dogs and was gone.

Ootek sat on alone. The wind, which had gusted so strongly and capriciously the night before, had completely died away, and the calm of the morning air was enveloped in a silence so profound he could hear his own heart beating. Then he heard another sound, faint and seeming far away. It was a sweet clear sound, which both charmed and soothed him. It was some time before he realized it was Kyloo singing to her baby.

7

The Meat of the Cat

Ootek now had a wife and son. He regarded them as his as surely as if he had won them in the usual way, for had he not found them and carried them to safety they would both be dead. Once the men of his kind had taken their brides by force, snatching them from their beds as they slept and carrying them off into the night, pursued by relatives intent on rescue. Among some tribes it was still the custom to re-enact this drama, although today it was more of a pantomime, the bride a willing accessory to the deed.

He felt a certain glow of satisfaction in the knowledge that he had carried off his woman in similar fashion, though it was death that had pursued them, not her family. No other bride had been carried away on the back of a deer and though he had not yet made her his bride, she had surely indicated her willingness to become one. The fact that her son was not of his blood line did not seem to him to be of the slightest importance.

Few families could be less well endowed with material goods. He had the clothes he stood up in, the skin tent in which Kyloo lay, the weapons and utensils he had made himself, and a shotgun he hardly dared to fire. He also had the caribou bull, and when Kyloo had recovered from the birth and was able walk again they could load their belongings on the bull's back and set off in search of a more suitable valley in which to spend the winter. Despite his confidence in himself he was not sure that this inland wilderness could supply all their needs, and their present shortage of food worried him a little

82

Once again he felt that intense longing for the sea, and the almost magnetic pull of the north. He was a child of starvation, yet he could remember, before the bad times came, when the people never lacked for food. Now, at this season of the year, there would be frozen seal meat buried beneath caches of stone, seal oil fermenting in skins, dried salmon berries, and *masru*, the Eskimo potato, packed in birchbark containers. There would be salmon and whitefish, dried and smoked, seabirds pickled in oil, and caribou meat, both frozen and dried. Then, when the long winter night came, the people would pass the time dancing and telling tales, secure in the knowledge that they would not starve.

His first priority then was to go hunting, and he wished that circumstance had not dropped him in this barren, windswept gorge. Few animals or birds would choose to make their home here, which meant that he would have to hunt further afield. Then a thought came to him. Only the previous night the caribou had carried him swiftly over a distance which, on foot, it would have taken twice as long to travel. Why not use the bull now, to journey to fresh hunting grounds?

Pausing only to tell Kyloo of his plans, Ootek collected his bow and arrows. For a moment his gaze rested on the shotgun, but it was heavy and unfamiliar in his hand, and he was not sure what effect the noise of it firing would have on the caribou. He left it where it lay, and slinging his snowshoes round his neck, went and untethered Anak. The big bull stood quietly and allowed him to mount, and then set off at a fast trot up the side of the hill. Since Ootek had no particular destination in mind, he gave the bull his head and let him travel freely.

He was searching for snowshoe hares, those ubiquitous rodents which were at times so numerous that whole populations ate themselves into starvation, or could be so elusive that a man might search all day with never a

83

sight of one. Their white winter coats blended perfectly with their surroundings, and even if one wandered on to a patch of ground swept bare by the wind it could easily be overlooked, or mistaken for a lingering patch of snow. The trick was to look for the eye, round and dark and glistening, like a berry dropped from the sky.

They crested the hill and began a gradual descent into a wide and treeless valley, the caribou's broad hooves gripping the snow, the tendons in his heels crackling all the while like hail falling on ice. Automatically Ootek glanced back from time to time to check his bearings, for it was easy to get lost in such a featureless expanse of land. He realized he had no need to worry. The caribou left a distinct trail it would be easy to follow.

Almost at once he saw a hare, quite close and seemingly unafraid, nibbling on some dried grass stalks that waved above the snow. Before he could fit an arrow to his bow however, Anak had moved on, and try as he might, Ootek could neither stop nor turn him. Anak was hungry and in search of good grazing.

He found it at last, and scraping away the snow with his hooves, he dropped his head and began to feed. Nothing Ootek could do in the way of kicking and prodding would divert him. Ootek sat astride him, frustrated and helpless, wondering whether to dismount and set off to hunt on foot. Then he saw another hare, again quite close and seemingly unafraid. This time Ootek was ready, and the hare died instantly, an arrow through its ribcage.

Sure in his mind that Anak would not be diverted from his feeding, Ootek slipped from his back and retrieved the hare. A small crimson rosette of blood stained the snow where the hare had died. Keeping one eye on Anak, Ootek strung the dead hare from his belt and began prospecting around, searching for fresh victims. First though he had to don his snowshoes, for the snow, though not deep, had drifted into the hollows of the land, and one false step could send him floundering up to his waist.

A long time passed but he sighted no more game, save for one hare squatting atop a ridge, which bolted long before he could get within bow shot. Gradually he drifted back to Anak, and mounted him, more to enjoy the warmth of his thick hide than for any other reason. Anak, having eaten his fill, moved off at a leisurely pace and almost immediately they came upon another hare, crouched down, its ears laid across its back, dozing in the thin sunlight.

Suddenly the truth of the matter dawned on Ootek. The hares instinctively fled from man, the predator, but a caribou wandering unconcernedly across the tundra presented no threat. Clad in furs, and half lying across the caribou's back, Ootek went unnoticed – until it was too late.

In a short space of time Ootek shot three more, each at close range. If future hunting forays were as easy and as successful as this one, they would not lack for food. Each hare was fat from summer feeding, and would make an ample meal for both, or rather the three of them. The skins, when dried and cut into strips, could be woven into a coverlet for the baby. Rabbit fur was regarded as the warmest of all. Or they could be used as socks. The pelt was stripped from the carcase like a sleeve, and left turned inside out to dry. Thus they became instant socks, to be worn until they grew too smelly, and were then thrown away.

Musing thus, while scanning the ground for more hares, it was with a faint shock of surprise that he came upon fresh caribou tracks in the snow. It was a moment before it dawned on him that he had swung round in a wide circle, and that the tracks he was studying had been made by his own beast. Chuckling at his own foolishness, he decided that perhaps it was time he returned to camp. He kicked his heels into Anak's flanks and set off back along the trail.

He had slept little the night before, and was still fatigued from his ordeal. The warmth that enveloped him from the deer and the rhythmic swinging motion of its stride lulled him into a half doze. From time to time he shook himself awake and looked ahead, checking to see they were still on the right trail. Ahead of him he saw a rock jutting above the snow cover.

He could not recall noticing it before, yet the track led straight towards it. He must have passed within arm's length of it. Anak plodded on, drawing ever nearer to the rock, and suddenly Ootek's pulse quickened as he recognized the greyish brown object for what it really was, a full-grown lynx crouching in the snow. It had found the blood from the first hare he had slain and was licking it.

He reached for an arrow and strung it to his bow. Lynx meat was good, as white and tender but better flavoured than the hares on which it fed. The pelt was prime too. It would make a hat and mitts, or a vest, or another coverlet for the baby. The lynx was within bow shot now, but Ootek held his fire, hoping that the cat would ignore the caribou as the hares had done, and let him get close enough to be sure of his aim.

Lynx and caribou saw each other instantaneously. Instead of fleeing, the cat gave a sudden snarl and poised itself to spring. Ootek's arrow flew from the bow, and at the same moment Anak gave a violent snort of terror and bolted, sending Ootek somersaulting over his rump, to land head over heels in the snow. Ootek caught a last view of the bull as it disappeared over the crest of the hill, shedding the hares Ootek had laid across its back.

The lynx was dying. Ootek's arrow had sunk deep into its neck where the throat entered the chest. It lay sprawled in the snow, one paw outstretched as though making one last attempt to strike. Ootek picked himself up and watched the fire go out of its eyes. After a while he leaned over and gently tapped one eye with the tip of

86

his bow. There was no reaction, and satisfied the lynx was dead he hefted it on to his shoulders and set off on foot to retrieve the hares.

A sixty-pound lynx carcase, and five hares averaging ten pounds apiece, made a considerable load for Ootek to pack, and it was a long way back to camp. All the way he fretted about the loss of Anak, and it was with great relief that he at last spied the bull loitering ahead of him, making his own way back to the camp site. Dusk was falling as Ootek reached the ravine and saw ahead of him the welcome glow of the camp fire. Kyloo had got up and was preparing a meal for them, the baby cradled in her parka hood.

Struggling to conceal his pride, Ootek strolled up to the fire and shrugged off the lynx, so that it flopped at Kyloo's feet. He had been brought up to understand that it was ill mannered for the hunter to show off, or boast about his kill, so he tried to assume nonchalance in front of Kyloo. All the same, he expected praise, so he was totally unprepared for the girl's reaction.

Instead of joy and delight at his success, Kyloo's expression was one of horror, and she recoiled from the dead lynx just as she had when Carver threw her the pouch of gold. Nothing Ootek could do would make her even go near the lynx, let alone touch it.

At first Ootek was completely unable to understand her. Only when he moved the carcase some distance away did she calm down sufficiently to be able to exclaim:

'*Hutlaanee! Hutlaanee*! It's taboo!'

After a while she explained that among her people the lynx was forbidden to women. They might not skin it, nor eat the meat, nor even speak its name, and great evil would befall them if they dared.

At last Ootek understood, but even so he could not conceal his disappointment. It was bad enough to be thrown from the caribou and land head over heels in a

87

snow drift. It was even worse to have to make the long journey back on foot, bowed down under the weight of the meat. Yet all the while his heart had been light at the thought of the rapturous welcome he would receive. The last thing he had expected was to have his gift spurned in such an outright manner.

After he had eaten he got up and began to skin the lynx. He refused to waste it, so he would eat the cat, and she could have the rabbit. Slowly his sense of humour returned, and as he thought of the spectacle he must have presented, flying backwards off the startled bull, he began to smile, and then to chuckle to himself. By the time he had finished his work he was his normal cheerful self again.

Watching him from across the fire Kyloo felt a warm glow of relief and contentment. Despite the misunderstanding over the lynx, this Eskimo boy was showing himself to be a good provider. He was kind and considerate, and even willing to risk his life on her behalf. Aaron had been kind enough, but he had never seemed to care how she felt or what she thought. Ootek was different, and after all he was not that much younger than she was herself. She resolved that as soon as she recovered from the birth of her baby she would give herself to him as a wife. Unless of course he took her first, a prospect that made her smile.

By morning it had begun to snow, and it continued through that day and all through the next, until the skin tent was all but buried in the drifts. Mercifully the wind was light, or their home might well have been destroyed. Despite the cold it was warm in the tent and there was little to do but sleep, and on waking to eat, or watch Tuktu lie naked on his back, kicking his fat little legs and clutching at his mother's hair.

In truth Ootek spent more time watching Kyloo than Tuktu. As she nestled among the folds of fur the satin sheen of her skin was enhanced by the silken lustre of the pelts, making Ootek's heart beat faster and his head

88

pound. From time to time, unable to resist the temptation, his hand strayed out to caress her, to cup the fullness of her breast in his palm and marvel at its weight, or to stroke the softness of her thigh. Though Kyloo made no move to encourage him, she made no attempt to resist. Instead she lay passive, resting on one elbow, her head cradled in her hand, surrendering to the sensual pleasure of his touch.

'You're beautiful,' he said.

Kyloo drew a lock of her dark hair across her face so that only her dark eyes showed above the veil. She was smiling, but a tear trembled on her lower lid and threatened to spill down her cheek.

'I'm lame,' she murmured.

'You're lame, and beautiful,' he replied. 'And when you are lying down, your lameness does not show.'

'But I can't lie down all the time,' Kyloo protested.

Ootek was silent for a long while. 'Be my wife,' he said suddenly. 'Be my wife, and you can lie on your couch, and I will bring you skins of marten and fox and otter and mink, and sit and look at you all day long.'

'And is that all we will do?' asked Kyloo slyly, and Ootek blushed and hid his face.

Outside, Anak patiently waited out the storm, sheltered in the grove of trees. By pacing to and fro he stamped out a yard, or corral, the walls of which gave him further shelter. The hard-packed snow beneath his hooves formed a raised platform from which he was able to browse on the branches of willow and aspen and poplar which had previously been out of reach. In consequence he fed better than before the coming of the snow.

On the morning of the second day Ootek donned his snowshoes and ventured outside. Overnight snow had obliterated the fireplace and buried their cooking pots, so after rescuing them he tramped around a bit, packing the snow down. Then he replenished their store of firewood and laid a platform of logs on the packed snow as a base

89

for a new fire. By then he was hungry, so he took off his snowshoes and crossed them to form a seat. He sat down and peered into the cooking pots.

They had been scrupulously careful to keep the lynx meat separate from the hare. Now, to his chagrin, he saw that whilst there was plenty of cat, most of the hare meat was gone. He stirred around in the soup, but only a few fragments came to light. There was plenty more hare hanging from the branch of a tree, but fifty yards of deep snow drifts lay between, and to cross them he would have to go through the performance of tying on his snowshoes once again. A sly thought crossed his mind. Kyloo was still asleep in the tent. She would be none the wiser if he shredded a small amount of the lynx meat and mixed it with the hare. It was indistinguishable in colour and texture, and the gravy would mask any slight difference in flavour.

Unsuspecting, Kyloo ate her breakfast without querying its content. Afterwards, Ootek felt slightly ashamed of his deception, and more than a little worried that the lynx meat might make her ill. He watched her closely for some hours but she showed no sign of any discomfort, and gradually he relaxed. All the same, he resolved never to play such a trick on her again.

It was five days before the weather cleared. Then one morning the sun hung low over the horizon, sending a brilliant light slanting across the snow. The air was crisp and clean after a heavy overnight frost, and there was not a breath of wind to stir the snow still clinging to the boughs of the spruce trees. Kyloo seemed rested and fit, and Ootek deemed it safe to move on.

They made slow progress at first. At times Ootek walked in front, breaking the trail with his snowshoes. When he grew weary he let Anak lead, but even the caribou's broad hooves would not always support him on the soft, drifted

90

snow, and at times he broke through, sinking almost to his chest. Kyloo limped along in the rear, struggling valiantly to keep up, but time and again she staggered off the narrow trail of trodden snow and floundered into drifts.

Though Ootek's heart was heavy at the sight of her suffering he dared not let her rest, for he knew that it was vital they should find somewhere secure to pass the dark days. They also needed a plentiful supply of meat to ensure they would not starve. A moose would serve to see them through until the spring, but he had seen no sign of one in all their journeying together. Looking back at Kyloo, a small bent figure trudging through the snow, he resolved to end her ordeal at the earliest opportunity.

Ahead lay a chain of mountains, their walls at first seeming low and distant under the clear blue sky, but gradually looming higher and more menacing as they approached. By the time they had climbed into the foothills Kyloo seemed exhausted, and though it was still early in the day it was clear she could go no further. In any case Ootek had no wish to spend the night camped high among those jagged peaks. The mountains spawned their own weather, and who knew what devil winds might arise, to sweep them off the mountainside. So he made camp, by a small stream close to a grove of aspen, and only when Kyloo and the baby were settled in comfortably did he set off alone to explore.

Since he had no inkling of what sort of terrain lay ahead he went on foot, guessing that before he found a pass through the mountains he might have to negotiate cliffs and rocks that the caribou could not cross. It was late in the day when he found what he sought and by then he was footsore and weary, and even his bones seemed to ache with the effort of wading through deep snow and scrambling over outcrops of stone. Even so he forced himself to go on, until he could stand at the crest of the ridge and look down at the land below.

At first he could only stand, holding his breath in reverence and awe. Then a wave of exultation and delight suffused his whole being, and he lifted his head to the sky and gave a great shout of joy and relief. The sun was setting, and the valley was suffused with a warm golden light. As soon as Ootek caught his first glimpse of it he knew that he would not find a better place in which to pass the winter. Spruce stood out dark against the snow. The twigs of the birch trees glowed wine red, and the thickets of poplar were suffused with pink. The river was frozen now, but Ootek knew that water still flowed beneath the ice, and there would be deep pools where Arctic char and grayling hid. There would be beaver and muskrat and snowshoe hare, and perhaps a moose or two. There was everything the wilderness could provide, food and firewood and shelter from the worst of the winter storms

Ten thousand years of patient toil had gone into the making of the land. Ever since the passing of the Ice Age, the river had crossed and re-crossed the valley floor, altering its course a hundred times. Each spring the melting snow sent flood water thundering down from the hills, breaking the ice and transforming the floes into countless battering rams which gouged away banks and felled mighty trees.

The flood water carried with it a load of gravel, sharp sand and silt, a cutting tool of immense abrasive power, gouging out pools, spreading gravel bars, sealing off an old channel so that it became a slough, saturating swampland and depositing a sediment of rich fertile silt in which fresh vegetation could thrive.

Here grew thickets of willow and alder, aspen, cotton-wood and spruce, spreading up from the gravel bars high on to the slopes of the hills. Above them grew berry thickets – blueberries, salmon berries, bear berries and wine berries – stands of fireweed and carpets of red sourdock. Higher still lay the mountain tundra, dwarf birch and prostrate willow, Labrador tea, moss campion, sedge tussocks and low bush cranberries.

Ootek stood for a while, drinking in the scene. Then he hurried down the mountain in the gathering dusk, eager to carry the good news.

Next morning he folded the tent early, and loading it on to the caribou's back he left Kyloo and the baby where they were and crossed the mountain alone. Later in the day he returned to collect them, and Kyloo made the last stage of the journey in comfort and ease.

They pitched their tent on a bluff overlooking the river, at the mouth of a narrow valley through which a small tributary stream still gurgled lazily beneath its mantle of ice. A tangle of driftwood, of every size from mature trees to tiny twigs, lay heaped along the shoreline, and close by a group of spruce trees gave shelter from the wind and a supply of soft bedding.

On the third day after their arrival Ootek found the fresh tracks of a moose. He had seen others previously, but they had all been old, made a day earlier at least, with hard-packed crusted snow glazed over them. These were fresh, the snow soft and feathery. Judging by the size they were made by a young cow, and the freshly bitten tips of a willow bough revealed where she had been feeding close by.

They led away from the river, up through the willow thicket, and followed a meandering course aslant the slope of the hill. The tracks showed that the moose was walking, not running, so, confident he had not frightened her, Ootek checked the direction of the wind. It blew from off the hill, so he headed back towards the river and swung round in a wide loop, being careful always to keep downwind.

Shortly he came upon the tracks again, and once more he circled round in a loop. He repeated this several times, moving fast on his snowshoes, but ever careful, when he felt he was drawing close to the trail, to approach with

93

caution, lest at the last minute the moose should become aware of his presence.

The short day was slipping by. The sun showed briefly above the mountains to the south, and then the valley sank into shadow again. Ootek was oblivious of the passing of time. His whole being was concentrated on the one thing that mattered for this moment in his life, the slaying of the moose.

At last, when he was sure he should have crossed the trail of the moose for the seventh time, the snow lay virgin and unmarked. Now there was nothing he could do but wait. The moose might have doubled back along its trail. It might have decided to lie up in some thicket. Otherwise, at any moment, it would pass his way. With the utmost stealth now, he began to work his way back towards where he guessed the moose might be.

Even so, he came upon it sooner than he expected, and for a brief instant he stood marvelling that a beast so huge could move so silently and remain so invisible in a setting in which he would not have supposed anything larger than a fox might hide. She was a cow, as he had hoped, and she stood slightly broadside on to him, nibbling unconcernedly on the bare twigs of an aspen.

His arrows were short, their heads minute, but the tips were razor sharp and the range was close enough for them to penetrate the toughest hide. He aimed at the point of the shoulder and heard the thud as the arrow buried itself between the ribs, sinking in up to the feathers. The cow started at the impact, lowered her head and gazed mildly at her flank, as if she had just been stung by a mosquito. Then she coughed once and moved forward.

Scarce daring to breathe, Ootek waited. He was sure his arrow tip had found her heart, and that already the life blood was flowing from it into her chest cavity. To panic her into running now could mean a long chase, and at the end of it the meat overheated and spoilt. So he stayed in

94

hiding and watched as the cow ambled past him.

When he judged the moose to be a safe distance in front of him he followed, and after about a hundred paces he saw from the tracks that she had begun to stagger. A few paces more and he saw her standing in front of him, swaying from side to side as she fought to overcome the weakness that had suddenly assailed her. Slowly she slid to the ground, her knees buckling beneath her and her breath escaping in a great sigh.

Ootek had killed his moose, but his day's work had barely begun, if he was to ensure himself of a supply of meat for the winter. Alone, and armed only with his hunting knife, he had to skin and butcher the carcase, dismembering it into joints he was able to handle.

With his snowshoes he dug a deep pit in the snow and lined it with the moose hide. Setting aside the tongue, heart, liver and kidneys, he set about disarticulating the hind legs from the pelvis. The forelegs were easier, but severing the head and dividing the backbone tried his patience and the keen edge of the knife, which despite his care dulled itself on the unyielding bone.

It was quite dark when he had finished. The time of the full moon had passed, and he had only the reflected light from the snow to aid him as he laid the meat in the pit and hacked down spruce branches to cover it. These in turn he covered with snow, stamped down hard so that when the whole mass froze it would discourage even the hungriest of wolves. By so doing he knew he was creating more labour for himself on the following day, when he would have to disinter the meat before transporting it back to camp. Yet he knew that it was necessary if the meat were to be properly protected.

The skin of the head, the lips roughly sewn together with thin strips of hide, made a pouch for the offal he had set aside. Thus loaded, he set off back to camp, and this time Kyloo welcomed the news of his kill with unfeigned delight.

Flushed with success, and filled with the fierce pride of the hunter, Ootek lifted her off her feet and carried her into the tent. There he stripped her of her robes and laid her on the couch, and this time he did not content himself with looking and stroking. Breathlessly, Kyloo surrendered to his demands, and it was some time before hunger of a different kind drove them from the tent.

Next morning, as soon as it was light enough to see, he caught up Anak, who was loitering by the river bank. In the absence of others of his kind, Anak seemed to have adopted the humans as his own, and never strayed far from the camp. He was now quite used to acting as a pack animal, and Ootek hoped to use him to transport the moose meat back to the camp. Yet as soon as Ootek had opened the pit and hacked away the covering of spruce branches with his axe, the smell of the meat threw Anak into a paroxysm of fear.

When Ootek attempted to load the hindquarters of the moose on Anak's back he started to rear and buck, kicking out with his hind legs and threatening to break the rawhide with which he was tethered to a tree. Nothing would induce him to calm down and accept them, and at length Ootek was forced to give in and abandon the idea.

The moose hide was frozen stiff at the bottom of the pit, hard and rigid as a board. Ootek lit a fire and hung the hide beside it to thaw out. While he waited he cut two slender spruce saplings and trimmed away the side branches until he had two smooth poles. He laid the thawed moose hide on the ground, hair side down, and rolled its edges around the larch poles, until he had formed a stretcher. He took melted snow and moss from around the fire and applied it in layers to the two poles, polishing and smoothing them as he worked. Then he left the hide to freeze solid again. When he turned it over he had a sledge.

Anak raised no objection to being harnessed to the sledge, even when it was loaded with meat. Fortunately the snow was hard packed and slippery, the going was even, and the way led downhill, so Ootek was able to move the entire supply of meat in one trip. From time to time the load slipped and joints tumbled off the sledge, but the frozen meat came to no harm in the snow, and it was an easy matter to reload.

By nightfall the winter supply of meat was stored safely under a cache of rocks beside the river, and the moose tongue simmered in a pot. Kyloo set half the ribcage of the moose to roast over a fire of hot coals, and laid strips of liver to fry in the fat that bubbled out of the meat. They gorged until their faces were shiny with grease, until the ribs were picked clean and the liver all gone.

In extreme cold the body demands an abundant supply of fuel if it is to function normally, so Ootek and Kyloo were not simply giving way to greed in eating so much. They needed the food to keep them warm. For some time now both of them had been suffering from a shortage of fat. Ootek had been reared on the coast, where for generations his people had harvested seal and walrus and the occasional whale, all sea mammals richly endowed with insulating layers of fat. Seal oil was a regular accompaniment to every meal.

Away from the coast the wilderness was a fat-starved land. Caribou were fat in the autumn. Some fish provided oil, and geese were fat. Sheep were another source, but they were scarce and hard to find, and so wary that they were difficult to hunt. So great was the demand for fat that the Indians and the inland Eskimo regularly traded with the coastal people, offering moose hides, which were scarce along the coast, in exchange for seal oil and blubber. Now, in addition to the meat, the moose carcase had yielded a good supply of fat.

From the ribs of the moose Ootek fashioned a two-pronged fishing spear, and carved a small fish, exact in every detail down to the fins and the scales on its back.

Then he cut a hole in the ice over a pool in the river. Lowering the carved fish into the water on the end of a line he jigged it up and down, causing it to flutter and dive, flashing in the clear water. Fish in the pool swam to the surface, attracted by the lure. Then, with a quick downward lunge, he tranfixed a fish between the tines of the spear and threw it out on to the ice, where it froze to death in an instant. After a while the surviving fish grew suspicious and refused to approach the bait. Then Ootek located another pool and cut another hole, where the fish were less wary.

Together they hunted for berries, still clinging to the bushes though buried under the snow. They also set snares for ptarmigan and hares, and made containers out of birchbark, spruce root and willow. Kyloo knew how to dress and tan skins, and she was expert with a needle. Her life so far, first with the fur trader and then with the gold miner, had prepared her well for life in the wild, yet there was always something new to learn, and Ootek was an adept and patient teacher – happy to have a new purpose now that he was no longer on the trail north.

With hare and ptarmigan, trout and grayling from the stream, berries, and moose meat from the cache, they now enjoyed a fairly varied diet. The moose grease they obtained from boiling the meat and bones was carefully skimmed from the top of the pan and stored in hare skins they hung from a nearby tree. Each skin held about half a gallon of oil. Some of it they used for preserving berries, and some they ate as a relish with their meat.

One night a wolf pack came down off the hill. They were a family of five, an old he-wolf, his mate, and three half-grown cubs, survivors of a litter of six. The summer had not been kind to the wolves, and by the end of it three of the litter had failed to make sufficient weight to survive the winter. One by one they had died, of cold and hunger and exhaustion. The others had barely managed to exist, and they were all lean and gaunt.

Anak was the first to be alerted by their presence, but even so they had almost surrounded him before he woke to instant flight. Close on his heels the pack raced in silent, grim pursuit, but Anak was stronger and faster than they. In a short space of time he had widened the gap between them so far that they grew discouraged and abandoned the chase, returning instead to the camp site where Ootek and Kyloo lay sleeping.

Here the smell of meat was strong, and hunger made the wolves bold enough to face the human scent that also lingered there. Ootek woke to a clatter as one of the wolves nosed over a pan left lying beside the fire. As he scrambled from the tent he caught a glimpse of a grey form in the flickering light of the dying flames, and he was just in time to see one of the wolves leaping up in an effort to reach one of the hare skins that hung from the tree.

With a shout that woke Kyloo and the baby he reached inside the tent for his bow and arrows, but by the time he had strung one to his bow the wolves had fled into the shadows beyond the fire. He waited a few moments, listening in the darkness, but the fretful sound of Tuktu wailing at being roused from his sleep masked all other sounds. Ootek bent and made up the fire with a handful of small sticks that crackled into a blaze, and in their light he saw a circle of eyes watching from the darkness.

He waited, bow in hand, but the wolf pack made no move. Then, as the flames died down the pack moved closer. Suddenly Ootek remembered the shotgun. Grabbing it out of the tent he broke it open, slipped two shells into the breech and then kicked the fire into life again. As flames and sparks leaped skyward he fired into the pair of eyes nearest the fire. The report of the gun was like a thunderclap in the stillness of the night, prompting Tuktu to fresh screams of outrage and sending the remaining wolves flying in terror from the scene. The old he-wolf lay dead, half his head blown away by the twin charge of shot. Ootek had pulled both triggers at once, and his shoulder was sorely bruised.

He waited a while but the wolves did not return, and he began to grow cold. Ruefully massaging his shoulder and arm he laid down the gun and crawled back into the warmth of the furs. The baby had ceased crying and had gone back to sleep. Beside him Kyloo stirred and slipped close to him, her hands caressing his face and brow. Ootek forgot about the wolves, and drew her into his arms.

8

The Keepers of the Game

Next morning the wolf carcase lay stiff and frozen in the snow, its head a shapeless mass of blood and brains and splinters of bone. Set rigid in the contortions of death, it would prove difficult to skin. Gently chiding himself for succumbing to Kyloo's charms rather than attending to it straight away, Ootek picked it up and hung it near the fire to thaw out a little. The wolf was a big one, and it took all his strength to lift it above his head. As he was admiring the luxurious black and silver pelt he wondered what had become of the rest of the pack, and then for the first time he remembered the caribou.

The big bull was nowhere to be found. Casting around, Ootek came upon tracks in the snow, and the story was plain for him to read. He saw where Anak had been ambushed by the wolves, and the flying hoof prints overtrodden by wolf tracks told of the chase. Then the paw prints turned off, and led back to the camp site, So at least Ootek knew that Anak was still alive, and in the absence of any bloodstains it was safe to assume that he was also unharmed.

As the hours passed and still the bull did not return to the camp, Ootek fretted and fidgeted for a while and finally set out to find the creature with whom he experienced such a strange bond. Because he did not expect to be gone more than a few hours he travelled light, taking only a few morsels of food, his hand axe and his bow. The trail he followed led away downriver, the tracks slowing to a brisk trot and then a walk. Ootek travelled fast, until despite the intense cold he began to feel hot, and slipped his parka back over his shoulders. All the while his eyes raked the distant landscape, hoping every moment to see the familiar form of the bull.

The days were very short now, the sun barely visible over the southern hills for just a few hours around noon. To compensate there were long hours of twilight, and the reflected light from the snow. Time and again in the dim light Ootek's eyes deceived him, and what he had thought to be the caribou turned out to be a low bush or an outcropping of rock.

When he began to feel chilled he realized that a thin, icy wind was blowing. Yet as he pulled his parka hood back up and hurried on, the wind grew stronger, panting in great icy blasts that pushed him sideways and clawed at his face and cheeks. Overhead the sky grew darker, and the peaks of the mountains were veiled from sight. Now it dawned on him that a blizzard was impending, and he knew that he ought to turn back and head for camp. Yet he also knew that heavy snow would obliterate the tracks he followed. Confident that, once found, the caribou would carry him swiftly back to camp, he increased his speed and pressed on.

Left to herself, Kyloo skinned the wolf and stretched the pelt on a framework of spruce branches. Then she cleansed her hands with snow and dried moss and stood for a moment gazing downriver, looking and hoping for Ootek's return. The breeze stirred the branches of the trees and blew cold on her face and she shivered in the silence. She built up the fire and crouched beside it for a while, but the breeze raised small clouds of ash and sparks that drifted into her hair, and the billowing smoke stung her eyes. She remembered the snares she had set. If it snowed, any birds or rabbits caught in them would be buried deep under the drifts.

She picked up the baby and tucked him into the back

of her parka. Taking a stout stick to aid her on her way and to kill any trapped game that might still be alive, she limped away up the hill. The first few snares were empty, but then in quick succession she found two that contained rabbits. She hung the corpses on a tree, not wishing to burden herself with them, and intending to collect them on her return.

Without Ootek's expert eye some of the snares were hard to find. Often she had to search for a long while before she suddenly spotted the one she was looking for, when all the while it had been close at hand. As yet she saw no need for urgency, but although the air was calm in the shelter of the woods, she could hear the wind above her moaning in the bare treetops, and the creak and groan of branches as they rubbed together.

At last she was confident she had found all the snares they had set in the woods. There remained those they had set for birds, higher up the hill beyond the treeline, where the berry bushes grew. It had not yet begun to snow. There was still time to check the snares if she hurried.

Beyond the trees the wind struck with a savagery that took her breath away. For most of the time it blew steadily, whipping the fur trim of her parka hood against her face, but every now and then she heard a great gust roaring up the valley. When it struck it threatened to whirl her away across the hillside, and she had to lean upon her stick and wait until its fury had passed.

She had barely reached the first ridge she must cross when she realized she could go no further. The gusts were more frequent now, and the icy chill they brought with them was such that her thick furs offered no protection against the blasts of icy air. Inside her parka Tuktu began to whimper and squirm, and she knew he too was suffering from the cold. With a quick pang of guilt she pulled him round so that he nestled against her breast, feeling his skin cold and clammy against her own. As she turned to retrace her footsteps the first snow came.

Away down the valley Ootek had at last located the straying caribou. Sensing the coming of the storm, the bull had taken refuge in a dense willow thicket that had sprung up round a fallen spruce tree. In falling, the roots of the tree had torn a great hollow out of the soft sandy soil. Anak lay in the depression, his back pressed against the root ball, and Ootek almost walked into him before he spotted him.

Despite all Ootek's efforts to persuade him, Anak refused to budge from his shelter. At last, worn out, tired, cold and hungry, Ootek conceded defeat. He knew that he could not make the journey back to camp on foot, and in any case he had no wish to abandon the bull. Kyloo was safe in camp, and though she might worry about his non-return, she would expect him to take shelter until the storm had passed.

Using one of his snowshoes he shovelled a space in the hollow clear of snow. Then he gathered dry wood and lit a good fire. While it was burning he collected more wood, cut a load of green spruce boughs and ate the meat he had brought with him. He had plenty of water to drink. He carried a skin bag under his robe, which at intervals he filled with snow. The warmth of his body melted the snow and kept the water from freezing until he needed to quench his thirst.

When the first fire was almost burned out he swept it to one side and rebuilt it close by. Then he spread the spruce boughs over the earth warmed by the first fire, curled up on them and fell fast asleep. Behind him Anak lay awake and watchful, suffused with the age-old patience of his kind, gazing into the flickering flames of the fire, while the snowflakes came dancing and whirling out of the night.

Across the hill, above the protective blanket of the trees, the blizzard roared with unchecked fury, a white wall of stinging blinding snow swept horizontal by an ice-laden wind now gusting at hurricane force. Twice Kyloo was blown to her knees. Each time she had to struggle to regain her feet, but she could only manage a few limping paces before the wind caught her and flung her across the side of the hill as though she weighed no more than a dried leaf.

The third time she fell she made no effort to get up. She lay sobbing for a while, gasping for breath and trying to force open her eyes so that she could get her bearings. Her only hope of shelter lay in the trees, but she looked in vain for the dark wall of the spruces. The white curtain of driven snow blotted everything from sight. In falling she had lost all sense of direction, but she knew that her way led downhill. Faint movements inside her parka told her that Tuktu still survived, and her one thought was to save him.

Slowly, grimly, she started to crawl through the drifts. If she stopped to rest the driven snow began at once to pile up against her, so fast that in the space of a few gasping breaths she was half buried, and had to fight and claw her way out of its clinging embrace. At first she had felt icy cold, but her hands and feet had been numb for some time, all sense of feeling lost. Now the numbness was spreading up her legs and arms, and when she tried to pull herself forward she had to concentrate on moving each limb. She was growing sleepy too, and waves of darkness came sweeping over her, like the great black wings of a bird.

A low shelf of rock barred her way, and lacking the strength to climb over, she crawled along its length a little way, until she came to a niche that offered some small shelter from the wind. She struggled to a sitting position, leaning back against the rock. Desperately she clutched Tuktu to her breast, sharing with him the last warmth of her body.

105

The driving snow swirled and eddied around her, clinging to her feet and legs, piling up until she was buried to the waist. She felt its gentle touch, like the furs that lined her couch, warm and soft and comforting. Soon Ootek would come, riding out of the storm on the back of his caribou bull. He would carry her back to camp and feed her hot soup. Then he would lay her on the couch and, like a little boy, stroke her legs and breasts and hair. Then the boy would become a man, and he would possess her, as he had done so many nights of late.

She wished he would come. They had enjoyed so short a time together, and she wanted to spend the rest of her life with him. She felt so tired lying there, and Tuktu was getting cold. She could no longer feel her feet and legs, and the cold was spreading up her thighs, like icy water rising all around her. Her last thought, as she lapsed into unconsciousness, was that she had left the hares hanging from a tree, and that they would be wasted if she did not retrieve them straight away.

Downriver Ootek waited for the storm to abate. For three days the snow fell, and even when the clouds began to break, the wind continued to blow with unabated ferocity, whipping up the fresh-fallen snow and sweeping it in stinging white veils across the land. To step outside the shelter of the willow thicket meant instant death from exposure.

As time passed it seemed to Ootek that he and the caribou were the last living things in a desolate frozen wilderness, where only the howling of the wind and the whisper of the driven snow broke the silence. No other game sheltered in the trees, no birds, no hares, not even a fox. Safe under the snow, he was sure, there was lesser game, mice and voles and ground squirrels, snug and safe in their burrows, but they were inaccessible to him.

106

Almost hourly the need for food, for sustenance of some sort, became more urgent. Much of the time he was able to spend sleeping, conserving vital energy, but the need to keep a fire going occupied most of his waking hours. The flames ate a prodigious amount of wood, and as he used up the fallen timber close at hand, he had to journey further and further afield.

Thirst was no problem, for there was plenty of snow. But hunger gnawed eternally, and as the days passed he grew steadily weaker. His one fear was that he would grow too weak to tend the fire, and die of exposure. A near accident with his axe, when the haft slipped from his grip and narrowly missed his foot, warned him of further danger, and reminded him that even if he survived the storm he could be too weak to ride back to camp.

To assuage his hunger he gathered fresh willow and spruce twigs and scraped the inner fibre from the bark, but it took a long while, and a lot of effort, to obtain more than a few handfuls. Even then, there was little nourishment to be gained, for the sap was not yet running and the sugar content of the bark was low.

Anak had no such problems. The bare twigs of the trees provided cellulose, which the bacteria in his gut were able to break down and convert into energy. All around him the branches of willow, birch and aspen were bitten back, the ends chewed and frayed. Watching him, Ootek knew that if he were to survive, the time was fast approaching when he must slay the bull.

Hourly, he delayed making the decision, hoping and praying that somehow the wilderness would come to his aid, to provide as it had done always in the past. At any moment a hare or a fox might appear, or a flock of birds blown on the wind. He cut a strip of hide from one of his boots and chewed on that. In the past his people had survived by cooking and eating their seal-skin boots, but he had nothing in which to boil his moccasins.

107

The sight of Anak began to haunt him, and resolutely he turned his back on the bull, staring instead into the fire. Yet even then visions of food continued to plague him, venison ribs roasting on the coals, thick steaks sizzling and broiling in the flames, soup bubbling in a pan, chunks of meat floating in a sea of golden glistening fat, liver and heart chopped fine and mixed with blood.

At the thought of blood he started visibly, his heart beat faster and he took a long, indrawn breath. An idea had occurred to him, a solution so simple he wondered why he had not thought of it before. He would only have one chance, and it would need infinite skill and care on his part. If it failed it would mean the death of the bull, but that was a risk he would have to take.

He rose to his feet, to discover he was shaking at the knees at the thought of what he was about to do. He picked up the rawhide reins and a short, stout stick. Struggling to control his nerves he approached the bull, and talking to him and fondling him all the while he took one end of the rein and tied him tight to a tree by the sawn-off stumps of his antlers. Then he took his knife and trimmed away a patch of hair at the bull's throat.

He tied a large knot in the other end of the rein and looped it round Anak's neck, positioning the knot over his jugular vein. Then with the stick he tightened the loop, slowly and ever so gently, until the vein stood out knotted and swollen below the loop.

All the while the bull had stood stoically suffering the operation without protest, but now he began to resist, and to jerk against the cord that held his head tight. It was now or never, and with a groan that was part prayer, part anguish, Ootek took his knife and stabbed it into the vein.

He had got it just right. The point of the knife just punctured the vein and did not pass right through, as

108

he had feared it might. A thin fountain of dark blood spouted out and fell on to the snow. Ootek let it flow until he judged he had enough, and then slackened off the tourniquet. At once the blood ceased to flow in such quantity, and died away to a thin trickle. Anak stopped struggling. The operation had, in fact, caused no more discomfort to him than the sting of a warble fly, and it was over in an instant. When Ootek released him he went back to feeding as though nothing had happened.

On hitting the snow the blood had frozen instantly, and Ootek was able to retrieve it in the form of a large, irregular black plate. The salty metallic taste was like nectar on his tongue, and after he had eaten about a third of it he set it carefully aside, well away from the warmth of the fire. Then he licked his fingers clean and scrubbed them in the snow to remove any last taint before going to check on Anak's wound. He need not have worried. The puncture was minute and had already sealed itself off. Ootek thanked him profusely and curled up on his bed of spruce boughs, where he fell fast asleep, his dreams unhaunted by visions of food.

At long last the wind softened and died, and travel was possible once more. Anak, seemingly unaffected by his loss of blood, suffered Ootek to mount, and together they set off through the drifts towards the camp. On the way Ootek sang to himself, his heart light at the thought of seeing Kyloo and the baby once more, and the prospect of stuffing himself to bursting on moose meat.

He found the camp deserted, the tent half buried in snow and the fireplace obliterated. Only the wolf skin, still securely lashed to its sprucewood frame, hung creaking in the light wind, mute evidence that someone once lived and worked here. For days he searched the valley and hill, repeatedly calling her name, but to no avail. He found the hares, still hanging from the tree, and once he passed within yards of where she lay, but the snow had buried her deep.

For a few days he loitered around the camp, but he knew, with a certainty that could not be denied, that he would never see her again. Worse, all the while he lingered, his grief was mingled with a feeling of dread. He believed in a spirit world, peopled by beings he knew only as the Keepers of the Game. Lest he should offend them, he had been brought up to respect all life, and even the corpses of the animals he killed. Unwittingly Kyloo had angered them, and he was to blame. He had fed her the meat of the cat.

9

The Village of the Dead

He had felt happy with Kyloo and the baby, happier than he had been since the famine, but now it was over, and he was alone again. Alone, except for the caribou, the bull which had won him his bride, which had carried him swiftly over the snow, the bull which had nourished him and given him back the gift of life. The caribou was all the family he had left now; and was father and mother and son to him. Yet always at the back of his mind was the fear, amounting to a certainty, that one day the bull would forsake him, to seek out the company of his own kind. Sooner or later a herd of wild caribou would cross their path, and the bull would answer their call.

He understood this, for he too yearned for an end to solitude. He longed for company, for the sound of laughter and voices, for the sight of friendly faces glowing round a fire. He still hungered for the taste and smell of the sea. One morning, gripped by new resolution, he folded his tent, packed his few belongings and set out to try to find Abner and the reindeer herd.

Since he knew they were heading north–east, and since the river flowed from that direction, he followed it. This was the way his people had travelled ever since his ancestors had crossed over from Asia during the last Ice Age. Throughout the brief summers they travelled the rivers by boat and canoe and raft. In winter they walked, and later journeyed by dog sled over the ice. A man was never lost beside a river. It gave him a sense of belonging, unlike the mountains and hills and the endless treeless plains. More importantly, it catered for his every need, water and wildfowl and fish and fuel, and sooner or later, game of every description, when it came to the water's edge to drink.

He did not know it, but Carver and Abner had chosen the same route, when they reached the river and found it frozen hard. The river saved them having to toil through the mountains, wandering in search of some unnamed pass which would guide them over the peaks. It saved them having to endure the blizzards and the ice-laden winds of the plains. The trees gave them shelter and provided winter browse for the deer.

The way was long, far longer than if he had just headed straight across country. The river twisted and curved, winding in great sweeping meanders, so that at times he might travel ten miles to cover one. Where there was a cut-off, and the going was easy, he took it, but more often the river was bounded by high banks or steep brush-covered bluffs.

There were hidden dangers too. The ice covering was not uniform, and water still flowed under the ice. Here and there, where the surface had frozen and the river level below had dropped, there were great caverns, roofed over by a thin coating of ice. Further on, the ice could be frozen down to the river bed, obstructing the flow of the water until it welled out over the surface. Any traveller attempting to cross this ran the risk of wet feet, and severe frostbite.

Anak seemed to have a sixth sense when it came to hollow ice, blowing clouds of white vapour from his nostrils and shaking his head as if in refusal before skirting round the danger area. Ootek trusted him implicitly in this, allowing him to have his way, even when the alternative was a scramble over snow-covered rocks or dense brush pitted with snow-filled hollows. It did not matter. Ootek was in no position to force their pace, and the river was all winter long.

Each bend, each twist and turn brought fresh vistas into view. High crags, haunt of peregrine, gyrfalcon and raven, towered in grey castellated pillars, the fissures in the rock etched white with snow. Rounded hills, pine clad, gave way to sloping walls of tumbling scree. Waterfalls, frozen until spring, shed a lace-like mantle of ice which flashed in the sun, now barely visible above the southern horizon. Though the sun was only visible for about two hours each noon, a long twilight period extended the day for another five.

At this time the moon was just as important a source of light as the sun. A half moon gave enough light to travel by, and the full moon shone for seven days at a time, circling endlessly in the sky, and its glow was bright enough to illuminate every detail of the landscape, even the distant mountains. On some nights the northern lights cast shimmering writhing curtains across the sky, suffusing a dull brightness that was reflected in the snow.

There were days when travel was impossible, or too arduous to contemplate, days of heavy ice fog, or high winds and blizzards. Extremely low temperatures altered the snow to devil snow, needle-sharp ice crystals that lacerated foot and hoof alike. Then there was nothing to do but eat and sleep.

The bond between Ootek and Anak grew stronger by the day. Without the bull Ootek would probably have gone mad, driven out of his mind by loneliness, grief and remorse. Anak, alone and isolated, deprived of the company and solace of his kind, clung to Ootek as the one familiar object in a strange and hostile environment.

Each day, towards the middle of the afternoon, Ootek started to look out for a suitable place to spend the night, one that would provide shelter, and browse for Anak. He no longer bothered to erect his tent of skins. If the weather was calm he would find a stand of spruce, and clear the snow from under a large tree. Here he would spread his

113

skins over a bed of green branches and keep a fire burning all night, so that the heat was reflected back under the tree. When the wind blew he dug a pit in the snow, with a raised bench lined with willow or spruce, and a roof of snow blocks.

For food he killed small game he encountered on his way. He had brought little with him from the camp. Their store of fat and the berries they had so laboriously gathered had all been stolen by birds and squirrels during the storm. He had long finished the moose meat he had brought with him, but though he often went hungry, he never starved.

Late one afternoon, as he rounded a bend in the river he came upon a trail leading up from the shore. It was so cunningly hidden, twisting up through a grove of willow, that had he stayed out on the ice he might have missed it. As it was, the first thing he noticed was the water hole cut near the bank, and he knew at once that the trail had been made by man.

He stood for a moment in the silence, listening and sniffing the air. There was a faint lingering smell of stale wood smoke and tanned hide, overlaid by a hint of decaying meat and ordure, but there was no noise, no laughter of children, no sound of anyone chopping wood. There was no smoke curling up from the trees, and no warning clamour of dogs. The water hole was frozen hard, clear sign that it had not been used for several days at least. The encampment appeared to be deserted. The people had probably moved on.

He hesitated for a moment. There seemed little point in exploring further, for he knew that if the people had left it was because all the available firewood had been burned, the bedding used up and the local game populations hunted out. There would be nothing except an evil-smelling litter of bones, offal and rags of hide. Nomads, he knew, often moved simply because the camp had become too insanitary for comfort.

Then at last his curiosity got the better of him, and he tethered Anak close to the river bank and set off up the trail. It wound and twisted through the bushes, and the slender leafless wands of willow were so dense that he could not see the clearing until he entered it. Then he stopped, and the hair on the back of his scalp prickled in a way he did not understand. A cluster of low skin tents stood huddled in one corner of the clearing. Meat still hung from the trees, and a flock of ravens flapped heavily away at his approach.

There was wood stacked neatly by the fire, ready for instant use, but the ash in the fireplace was cold. A hide cooking vessel hung from a tripod nearby. Obviously the people, whoever they were, still cooked in the old way, by heating stones red hot and plunging them into water until it boiled. Everywhere a dusting of fine powdered snow showed that no one had been near the fire that day.

Nervously Ootek approached the first tent and lifted the flap. The sleeping couches were still there, and the usual litter of belongings: moccasins, a bowl and spoon carved from birchwood, a bow and arrows, a stone axe, a lamp complete with oil and wick. It was as if the occupants had just left their beds, walked out, and failed to return.

One by one Ootek checked the other dwellings. Each told the same story. The occupants had left, without taking any of their possessions except the clothes they were wearing at the time. He came to the last tent and pulled back the flap. Inside lay the bodies of three people, still wrapped in their sleeping robes.

Gingerly Ootek lifted a corner of the robe that covered the nearest corpse. The face was covered in scabs, so closely clustered that one overlapped the other. The eyes were sealed with crusted yellow matter, the gaping mouth ulcerated and raw. Ootek dropped the robe and fled, not stopping until he was well away from the tent. It occurred to him then that he was not sure whether the corpse was that of a man or a woman. The face was too badly destroyed.

It was clear to him now that the people had become infected with some foul disease, one that killed them as they lay on their beds. But where were the others? Ootek could understand the people abandoning the sick ones to their fate, but they would not simply walk away, in the depth of winter, without shelter or possessions of any kind.

He found the answer a little further up the hill where eleven bodies lay in the snow. Three others had been given a decent burial, with cairns of stones built over their graves. Ootek guessed that when the disease had first struck, the people had held proper funerals for the victims, but as the illness spread and more and more fell sick, they became too weak and ill to administer to their dead.

Slowly Ootek walked away from the encampment, and retraced his steps back to the river. There was nothing he could do to help. Eventually the eagles and the ravens would pick the corpses clean, and their bones would be scattered by the foxes and wolves. The tents would moulder under the summer sun and rain, the tent poles would rot under their weight. Slowly the contents would crumble into dust and become one again with the earth. In a few summers all trace of the people would be gone from the face of the earth, with only a few axe heads and arrow heads remaining, buried deep in the soil.

He had not handled any of the corpses. He had touched nothing except with his gloved hand. He took nothing from any of the lodges, and left behind a small fortune in fine furs, otter and mink and fisher and fox, wolf, beaver, muskrat and ermine. He had learned, from Carver, the value of such goods, but fear of what might befall him if he robbed the dead of so much as a single pelt made him desist.

That night, as he lay wrapped in his cocoon of skins, gazing into the red glow of the fire, he thought about the village of the dead, and wondered what evil forces had struck them down. He was not to know that smallpox was one of the most infectious and deadly diseases known to man. Once introduced into the New World it spread with terrifying speed, carried on bedding, blankets and clothing as well as by direct contact. Since twelve or fourteen days could pass between the initial infection and the onset of illness, and since a man with a good dog team might travel fifty miles in a day, he could carry the germ more than six hundred miles before passing on the disease. Most of the victims died without ever seeing or even knowing about the existence of the white men who first brought the plague.

He could only assume that the people had been guilty of some terrible crime to have suffered such a fate. It was well known that those who showed disrespect for the corpses of animals they had killed suffered bad luck as a result. He remembered one man who had tripped over the severed head of a bear. He had turned and kicked the head, and called the bear names. Soon after he had fallen and broken his leg. Another man caught a raven and threw it alive to his dogs. The dogs died, and he suffered bad luck in his hunting for the rest of that year.

Yet try as he might he could not imagine anything bad enough to bring about the death of a whole village. Most unfortunate were those who had not been awarded a proper burial, for their spirits would not be able to rest and would be condemned to wander the woods for all eternity, trying in vain to join the living again, haunting fishing camps and hunting parties, or following lone travellers in the night. Ootek could only pray that he had not inadvertently angered the spirits, and he was glad he had put a good distance between himself and the camp. Even so, it was a long time before sleep came that night, and his dreams were tormented by visions of faceless men.

During the next few days he travelled hard and fast. The horror of his encounter had left him, only to be replaced

117

with a dull despair in which he imagined he was the only human left alive in an empty and silent wilderness. With every waking moment he found himself longing for the sound of other voices, for laughter, for the companionship of his fellow men. He even found himself remembering with affection his days with the Nunamiut, although at the time he had felt isolated and alone. Now he was beginning to know the meaning of true solitude. He had lost all sense of time. He had not the slightest idea of where he was, and he was beginning to lose his identity. One morning, on waking, he forgot which side of the river he had spent the night on, and travelled several miles back along the route he had followed the day previously, before the position of the sun alerted him to his mistake.

The realization further depressed him. Worse, he found he was losing his strength, and though he fought against this at first he gradually gave way to his lassitude, sleeping longer in the mornings and retiring earlier at night. A bad gash on his thumb, where he had cut himself dismembering a hare, steadfastly refused to heal. One blustery night, as he was attempting to kindle a fire, he had a sudden nose bleed.

The sight of the blood, a spattering of bright blossoms on the snow, so terrified him that he was unable to eat or sleep at all that night. Instead he sat hugging his knees and staring out into the darkness. He was now quite certain that the plague which had visited the village of the dead had at last descended on him. It was only a matter of time before his face was eaten away, his corpse left stiff and forgotten in the snow and his spirit set free to wander for ever over the frozen land.

10

The Gift of the Wolverine

The big dog growled deep in his throat, but so softly that Carver, who stood right beside him, could barely hear him. Immediately he stopped dead in his tracks. Handsome only made that sound in the presence of big game. Now the dog's lips were bared in a noiseless snarl and the hairs along the ridge of his spine were raised as he gazed fixedly at a dense patch of undergrowth close by the river bank.

Carver badly needed a moose, or a caribou, and if he did not find one soon he knew they would have to slaughter one of their reindeer. This would be a pity, for the young bulls they had castrated in the autumn were fattening nicely. Yet for some time now both moose and caribou had been hard to find. Maybe the cold had driven them farther south, or maybe the terrain was not quite to their liking.

He stared hard at the thicket, but for a long time he could see nothing. This did not surprise him, for he knew how easily a large animal could hide in cover so sparse that seemingly it would not even conceal a hare. Instead he trusted Handsome, for he had seldom known the dog to be wrong in such matters. So he waited and watched, and after a while he saw a bush move, although no wind stirred. It was the merest flicker of movement, a twig bending and then springing upright, but he knew then that a large herbivore was feeding there.

Now he concentrated his gaze on that spot, and after a moment he saw that what he had taken for a branch was in fact the outline of a shoulder and foreleg. Infinitely slowly he slid his rifle from his shoulder, thumbed back the safety catch and eased a bullet into the breech. He knew that the faintest click would echo across the cold clear air and alert his prey to instant flight.

He estimated the range at about a hundred yards, and the sun was at his back. At that range he could not possibly miss, but still he held his fire, debating which would make the most successful shot. A shoulder shot would bring the animal down, but it would waste a lot of meat. A heart shot would be better, but even a mortally wounded moose could run a long way before it died. A neck shot was best, but for that his aim had to be deadly accurate, or the animal would only be slightly hurt. He waited until he could get a clearer view.

As if in answer to his prayer the animal stepped into sight. Carver glimpsed the thick neck and the creamy white cape that overlaid the shoulder pad, and knew that what Handsome had found was a magnificent caribou bull. The head was clearly visible now, the muscles rippling on the sleek dark neck, and Carver levelled his sights. Gently his finger closed round the trigger. Another pound of pressure, and the heavy bullet would shatter the bones of the neck and the spinal cord would be severed. Then suddenly he lowered the gun.

At the last instant before he pulled the trigger he had seen something that made him gasp for breath and then exhale in a long slow whistle. Instead of the magnificent spread of antlers he had expected to see on the caribou, this bull was adorned with nothing more than two short stumps. Carver knew there could only be one animal within a hundred miles that had been mutilated in such a manner. Had the beast gone wild, or was Ootek the Eskimo also close by? He flipped over the safety catch and slung the rifle back across his shoulder. Then with Handsome grumbling at his heel he set off towards the thicket.

By the time he had covered the short distance the caribou had gone. Once he caught a glimpse of it, drifting like a trace of wind-blown smoke through the trees before the wilderness swallowed it up. The cover was denser and more widespread than he had first realized, a tangle of willow and poplar clinging precariously to the steep hillside and clothing the ground as far down as the river. Twice he called Ootek's name, his voice seeming unnaturally loud in the silence, but though he listened for a long while no answer came.

Then he glimpsed the caribou again. It was standing just a little way ahead, watching him warily, as if curious yet poised for instant flight. As Carver approached it vanished again, almost as if inviting him to follow, so now Carver put Handsome on a leash and let his nose do the work.

They found Ootek lying in a hollow beneath some rounded boulders, almost on the river's brink. He stared up at them with vacant, unseeing eyes, but as Handsome strained towards him, wagging his tail in recognition of an old friend, Carver saw the eyes blink, and Ootek stirred.

There was a fire smouldering close by, but no stocks of wood to replenish it. There was a cooking pot, but no food. Carver kicked the logs together so that they burst into flame, then knelt and put his arm round Ootek, raising him to a half-sitting position.

'Looks like we found you just in time,' he murmured.

Ootek was icy cold, his pulse weak and rapid, his skin clammy to the touch, but as far as Carver could see there were no injuries. He laid him down again and busied himself collecting wood, replenishing the fire and packing the cooking pot with clean snow. Then while the water heated he massaged Ootek as hard as he could, chafing his limbs and slapping his cheeks in an effort to restore his circulation. He had a supply of pemmican with him, and when the water was hot he threw the mixture of meat, berries and fat into the pot and stirred it into a soup.

At first Ootek refused to drink, but then Carver lost patience, and seizing Ootek by the back of the neck he thrust the pan roughly against his lips so that it clashed against his teeth.

'Come on, you no-good worthless Siwash,' he growled. 'Does it need a white man to teach you how to survive in your own country?'

Whether it was the insult, or merely the threatening tone of his voice, Carver was not sure. What mattered was that it worked, and after a moment Ootek began to gulp greedily at the mixture. At first Carver let him have his way, but after a few swallows he pulled the pan away and laid Ootek back on the skins. He did not want his precious broth thrown up before it had a chance to do some good.

The fire burned brightly now, its flames radiating back to warm the two men. After a while Ootek sat up of his own accord and reached for the soup once more. This time he drank slowly, taking small sips and pausing between each one as he told Carver some of the events that had passed since they had parted. Carver's eyes narrowed when Ootek described his visit to the village of the dead, but he said nothing, waiting patiently until Ootek had finished his tale.

Then, 'How long since you found the bodies?' he asked.

Ootek tried to think. He seemed to have been wandering for so long, and he had never been good at counting the days. 'The moon had just ripened at the time,' he said. 'Now it is full again.'

Carver heaved a sigh of relief. He well knew the terrible consequences of coming in contact with cases of smallpox, but he guessed that if Ootek had been infected he would be dead by now. He was suffering from semi-starvation, and in particular a form of scurvy due to a diet consisting almost entirely of meat. He also had a touch of frostbite, but he hadn't got smallpox.

'How far is it to your camp?' asked Ootek. His old enmity with Carver was forgotten in his relief at being rescued. Carver for his part seemed to bear him no ill will. Ootek naturally assumed, without being invited, that he would join up with the others as before and continue the journey north.

Carver shrugged. 'A few hours. Half a day at most, but you're not fit to walk it. Best lie here, and I'll go back and harness up the dog team.'

'There's no need.' Ootek pointed beyond the clearing where he lay, and Carver saw that the caribou had reappeared and was standing in the bushes, regarding them with an air of mild curiosity. 'I can ride,' Ootek said.

Abner was both astonished and delighted to see the small procession walk into camp that night. At the sight of Ootek's grinning face he realized how much he had missed the boy, and as they sat round the fire after supper that night he insisted on hearing every detail of Ootek's adventures. He was a little concerned though to learn that Carver had failed yet again to find meat, especially now that there was another mouth to feed.

'The boy is going to need feeding up if he is to grow strong again,' he said. 'Maybe we ought to kill one of the deer.'

Carver stared reflectively out over the herd grazing quietly in the valley below. 'Be a pity to kill any of those reindeer steers,' he remarked. 'They ain't cost us nothing to raise, yet they got to be worth anything up to a hundred dollars apiece. If ever we can find a market for them, that is.' He sighed, and knocked out his pipe. 'Still, if things get desperate we can always knock one down. It'll be an expensive meal, but there it is.'

He chuckled and waved the stem of his pipe at Anak, who had rejoined the herd and was placidly grazing alongside the others as if he'd never been away. 'If you hadn't sawn the antlers off that there bull, we'd be eating caribou tonight. I came within a split second of shooting him.'

123

'*You* would be eating caribou,' corrected Ootek. 'I would be dead.' He lay by the fire, looking more like his old relaxed and cheerful self. Good food and companionship were all that was needed to jolt him out of his lethargy. Already he felt stronger, and he had begun to think that perhaps he was not yet meant to die. If he had been, then the spirits would not have sent Carver to find him. Again it seemed that he owed the caribou his life, for had it not been for Anak, Carver could well have passed by the spot where he lay. There and then he took a silent vow never to kill another wild caribou as long as he lived. Being essentially practical in his outlook, however, he was careful not to foreswear the eating of caribou meat.

Slowly the winter was passing. The days were steadily lengthening, though snow still lay deep on the ground and the river remained frozen hard. Since it still led roughly north and east they stayed with it, and at the end of each day's travel, when the herd rested and fed, Ootek took the opportunity to go foraging again. Partly because he craved their sweetness, and partly because they made a welcome addition to the diet, he spent long hours combing the hillsides that bordered the river, knocking the snow off the berry bushes and finding those fruits that had been missed in the autumn. The extreme cold enhanced their flavour, concentrating the juices that had formed under the summer sun, and since he ate as many as he picked, the berries speeded his recovery.

It was while he was prospecting for a fresh berry patch that he came upon the wolverine tracks, and since they were fresh he followed them, for the pelt of the wolverine was much prized.

The tracks led up and across the hill for several miles, and Ootek began to grow weary. Then, just as he had decided that the wolverine was moving too fast and that he would never catch up with it, he noticed that at one point the trail turned aside. It led to a small hummock in the snow, but then it continued on, to disappear over the summit of the hill. Something, it was clear, had attracted the wolverine's attention and diverted it from its path just long enough to investigate the site.

There was nothing to be seen except a yellowing in the snow, with a small hole in the centre. At first Ootek thought that the wolverine had urinated there, but when he looked closer he saw that whatever it was that had melted the snow came from underneath. With a growing sense of excitement he realized that the wolverine had led him to a bear den. Next moment, his weariness forgotten, he was racing back down the hill to inform the others.

They took their guns, and axes, and several long, curving wands of willow. When they had cleared away the snow they saw that it was indeed a bear den, its entrance securely blocked with frozen earth, grass, rocks and other debris, with just a small breathing hole at the top.

'Grizzly!' muttered Carver, and the others nodded thoughtfully.

It made a difference. Both black and brown bears lived hereabouts, but black bears were known to sleep soundly, so profoundly that a hibernating black bear could sometimes be dragged out by its heels before it awoke. A grizzly, on the other hand, was a much lighter sleeper, and anyone disturbing its den was liable to be interrupted in his work by the sudden explosive appearance of a very wide awake and angry bear.

With these thoughts very much in mind, Carver and Abner took up station one on either side of the entrance, their rifles at the ready. Ootek lay in the snow above the breathing hole and very gently slid one of the willow wands into it. At first he could feel nothing, but then, when almost the full length of the wand had been pushed through, he encountered a soft resistance.

Withdrawing the wand, he laid it on the ground along the same line of direction it had followed inside the hole.

Now they knew the bear lay exactly under the tip of the wand. While Carver continued to guard the exit, Abner and Ootek began to dig down through the frozen earth with their axes, and before long they had broken through the roof of the den.

As the last fragments of earth rained down on the sleeping bear it stirred, and a low, angry growl issued from the darkness below. Each man held his breath, Carver in particular expecting to see the earth wall in front of the den disintegrate, torn apart by the fury of the bear. Nothing happened however.

After a prolonged wait Abner tried to peer down through the hole. It was no more than six inches square, and the den was very dark, so that although he could see the bear he was uncertain which way it lay.

Carver chuckled when he heard this. 'Don't shoot it in the backside if you want it to stay friendly,' he called.

Gingerly Abner set about making the hole larger. Only the upper layer of earth was frozen hard. The warmth of the bear below had kept the sand at the roof of the cave soft and crumbly. He worked with infinite care, taking just a handful at a time, and stopping every time the bear stirred. At length Carver grew impatient with the progress that was being made, and climbing up to the top of the den he brushed Abner aside and peered down through the hole.

At that precise moment the bear woke, and finding its shelter desecrated, thrust its muzzle into the hole. Carver heard the roar and found himself staring into the bear's open mouth, his face only a foot away from the glistening yellow fangs. He jerked backwards, and as the bear began to withdraw its head from the opening Carver seized his rifle and shot it between the eyes.

After that the hard work began, as they tore away the debris that blocked the entrance and dragged the bear into the light. It was a young male in the prime of life, as fat as it had been on the autumn day when it crawled into its den and began its last long sleep. They hauled the corpse on to a patch of clean snow, where Abner and Ootek set about skinning it while Carver went to get his dog team and sledge.

Abner removed the bear's paws from the carcase and slit the eyeballs. This was to ensure that the spirit of the bear could not see his killers, nor pursue them back to the camp. The paws would not be wasted however, but grilled over the fire and eaten.

The dogs got the liver and lungs and part of the intestines. The rest they saved, for bear meat was a great delicacy. That night they prepared a feast. They turned the stomach inside out and stuffed it with chopped meat, heart, and a liberal helping of lacy fat from the mesenteric apron that covered the intestines. Then they tied the openings and roasted the stomach over the fire. The bear's paws were put to grill over hot coals, and when all had been eaten they sat around frying lengths of intestine they had threaded on long sticks.

With the grease running down his chin, Carver waved his sausage in a gesture of thanks to Ootek. 'Seems like your hide was worth saving after all,' he remarked.

'It was the wolverine who led me to the den,' replied Ootek modestly, but all the same he felt a glow of pride at his achievement. That night as he fell asleep he felt happier and more secure than he had done for a long time.

11

River Journey

For some time now Carver had been growing restless. As day followed day and the herd wound its slow twisting way north, following the line of the river, he became more and more impatient with the rate of progress. On a good day they might cover fifteen miles. More often it was ten, or merely five. There were mornings when the herd was scattered far and wide, and it took until noon to round them up and get them on the move. There were days when they did not travel at all. Even on the best days they travelled twice or even three times the distance between two points.

Despite Carver's urging, despite his pleas for an early start, or his attempts to prolong the journey at the end of the day Abner would not allow the herd to be hurried. Early each afternoon he began to watch out for a place where there was plenty of browse for the deer and driftwood for a fire. As soon as he found somewhere suitable, then no matter how much Carver fretted and fumed, there he would stop for the night.

In an attempt to shorten some of the delays, and also to relieve his frustration, Carver took to prospecting ahead, finding short cuts across some of the wider bends of the river and locating camp sites further upstream that he felt would meet with Abner's approval. By this means he was able to increase the distance they travelled each day, if only by a few miles.

Late one afternoon, when the herd had come to rest and the others were setting up camp, Carver whipped up his dog team and headed far up the river. As always he sensed a feeling of freedom and power in travelling at speed over the snow, for he had come to enjoy these solitary excursions for their own sake, regardless of any purpose they might serve. So he travelled further than usual, knowing that although night would soon fall there was a bright moon to guide him safely back to camp. He rounded a bend in the river, and there, not far from the shoreline, stood a small cabin set snug beneath the trees. A plume of thin grey smoke issuing from its tin stove pipe showed it was occupied.

Carver slowed his team to a stop and stood staring with astonishment and a mounting sense of excitement. It had been well over a year since he had last spoken to another white man, and his desire, now that the opportunity presented itself, was overwhelming. To his surprise he found himself trembling. He whipped up his team again and drove them slowly towards the cabin, cracking his whip and shouting, more to alert the occupant of his presence than to guide them.

There was a clamour of dogs from somewhere behind the cabin. He saw a flicker of movement at the tiny window and watched the door open a crack. The muzzle of a rifle glinted in the light. Then a round face framed by a bushy black beard emerged and broke into a broad grin. The rifle was lowered, and a few moments later Carver found himself seated inside the cabin, sipping scalding black coffee from a tin mug.

The man's name, he learned, was Jean Paul. His mother had been French, and he had drifted into the territory from Canada some years before. He was a fur trapper like Carver, one of a new breed of men who were learning how best to exploit what still remained of the once rich harvest of soft gold. He kept a team of fifteen dogs, which enabled him to travel far and fast, and he ran two traplines, each covering a tortuous circuit almost three hundred miles long. Only in this way could he trap enough fur to make

129

the work pay. Times had been hard, he admitted, but now they were improving. More fur bearers were to be found, and he showed Carver some of the pelts he had cleaned and dried.

Carver fingered the silky black fur of the marten he was holding, and measured the length of the guard hairs. 'Where do you sell your skins?' he queried.

'Downriver,' said Jean Paul. 'Oh! Not this river,' he exclaimed as Carver looked up in surprise. 'Across the hills to the west. There's another, broad, flat, flows west to the sea. There's a trader there. Sails upriver each summer. Arrives in the fall, stays all winter, and leaves as soon as the ice breaks in the spring. Funny little chap, but a straight arrow. He'll either buy for gold, or trade goods.'

Carver mulled over this information in silence for a while. Over the year, in addition to a number of moose hides he had amassed a good store of pelts – fox, fisher, muskrat, otter and lynx – and now he had the bear skin to add to the pile. He could not keep them indefinitely. Already some of the earlier ones had started to deteriorate. Now was the time to dispose of the others, before the warmer weather came and spoiled still more.

They were also fast running out of supplies, especially salt, tea and tobacco. Already they were drying tea leaves and brewing them over again, until no amount of stewing would colour the water in which they were boiled. Their supply of sugar was long gone, and they were mixing their meagre store of tobacco with dead willow leaves and bark.

He was also badly in need of a new set of clothes. There was a limit to the amount of patching and repair the best of skins would stand, and come the spring, when the warmer weather arrived, he would start to smell worse than he did now.

'How far to this trader?' he queried.

Jean Paul shrugged. 'Three days. Maybe four,' he replied.

Mentally Carver doubled the figure. It would take his small team twice as long to cover the distance. To divert the reindeer was out of the question. They were much too slow, but he could be gone a month or more and still catch them up on their long journey north.

There was one small problem to overcome, and that was the question of food. In addition to his own needs, Carver would require food for his dogs before undertaking a journey of this nature. Travelling with the herd, and covering only a few miles each day, they needed little more than a pound of meat each evening to keep them in condition. Many a time they got less than that. Out on the trail, and working hard in the cold, they would require at least twice that much, and maybe more. Even though the sledge would be lightly loaded, Carver would need at least a hundred and fifty pounds of food for a week's travel, and he could hardly ask Abner and Ootek to give up so large a share of the bear.

Carver stayed late into the night chatting with Jean Paul, and in the morning he outlined his plans to the others. As he had feared, they viewed the idea of feeding so large a portion of the bear to the dogs with considerable dismay. Although Carver had shot the bear, Ootek had found it, so Carver had little option but to respect their wishes. Instead, it was agreed that they go on a moose hunt, travelling as light as possible, and staying out overnight if need be.

At first it was planned that all three should go, but during that night they were awakened by a wolf pack howling nearby. By the volume of the sound they judged it to be a large one, and next morning Abner fretted about the safety of the reindeer herd if it was left unguarded. Ootek volunteered to stay behind in camp, so soon after breakfast Abner and Carver set off, taking only their rifles, some food and a sleeping robe apiece. Handsome followed at Carver's heel.

By the end of the second day, dejected and weary, they stood close to an alder thicket about a mile upstream from the camp, waiting to see if Handsome could flush a moose out of the trees. They had swung in a great circle, crossing the nearest hills and working their way up a narrow wooded creek that lay like a great jagged wound across the land. On several occasions they had found sign of moose, but each time the trail was old, the hoof prints glazed over, the piles of droppings frozen like great bunches of golden grapes in the snow. One set of tracks, judging by the size of them, had been made by a huge bull, and Carver's finger was itchy on the trigger, for he knew that an angry bull moose could be as dangerous as a charging bear.

The thicket was empty however. After a long wait Handsome emerged on to the ice, shaking the snow from his muzzle, his ears laid back, his tail hanging low, sure signs that he had drawn a blank.

Carver shouldered his rifle. 'What now?' he muttered.

Already the light was failing. The prospect of another night out in the bush, when camp lay so near to hand, did not appeal to either man. Grudgingly Carver acknowledged defeat, but at that moment a distant report rang out. It echoed and re-echoed among the hills, so Carver couldn't be sure whether it was one shot or two, but he immediately thought of Ootek alone back in the camp.

'Wolves?' he queried, but Abner was already heading down river.

The deer herd was scattered the length of the valley, pawing the snow and grazing as though nothing untoward had occurred. In the camp there was a strong smell of singed hair, and the body of a huge moose lay sprawled across the fire. Ootek sat on its rump, grinning broadly and rubbing his shoulder with his left hand.

132

'A moose came to warm himself by the fire,' he announced. 'I shot him from the tent.'

There was a hole the size of an orange in the moose's side, just behind the shoulder blade. Carver stared at it with mixed feelings of admiration and dismay.

'You sure did,' he remarked. 'Good job you ain't got more than two barrels on that scatter gun. There'd be nothing left but the hide, and even that wouldn't keep out the rain.'

Ootek ignored the jibe. 'Now you have moose meat for your dogs,' he announced. 'Have a safe journey.' He waved his arm in a lordly gesture, and Carver bowed and acknowledged the gift with thanks.

That night they dined on moose ribs liberally salted with shot, and amused themselves seeing how far they could spit the pellets they found embedded in the meat. The rest of the carcase was undamaged, and next morning Carver loaded his sledge with a cargo of pelts, and two hundred pounds of moose meat to feed him and his dogs for the journey. A mountain of meat still remained, to sustain the others while he was gone.

On the first day he made forty-five miles, and could perhaps have gone further if the dogs had not been soft from lack of exercise. Hard-packed snow, firmed by the wind, covered the surface of the land, so Carver had no need to walk ahead of his team, breaking a trail with his snowshoes. Instead he could ride behind, standing on the runners of his sledge as the dogs raced ahead. Jean Paul had given him careful instructions as to the route he had to follow, and sure enough, by evening he could see the river ahead, gleaming in the light of the setting sun.

He camped that night on a gravel bar well out in mid stream, where a small stand of young pines had taken root. A great wall of driftwood had built up against them on the upstream side of the island, carried there by the previous spring floods. One day another flood would sweep down and carry away driftwood, pines and island, but for the moment it offered a snug sheltered haven from the wind.

Almost as an afterthought he had brought along the two Colt pistols he had inherited from the dead miner, sticking them in his belt, hidden under his parka. They had proved so heavy and uncomfortable to wear that after a while he had halted the team and stowed the pistols on the sledge. Now, after he had dined on moose liver and sausage, grilled over the coals of his fire, he occupied himself making a pair of rawhide holsters from a piece of moose-hide. One day, he promised himself, Alaska would have laws, and people to enforce them. Meantime he had no wish to be surprised and robbed, either by Indians or white men.

During the next two days he made even better progress as the dogs settled into the routine and grew hardened to the work. The weather held fine and their load was light, and each morning they crawled from the holes they had dug in the snow, to greet Carver with furiously wagging tails and a chorus of delighted barks.

Throughout that whole time Carver saw no other living soul, nor any sign of habitation. On the fourth day out a wind began to blow, and seeing the snow whipped off the mountain peaks to the north Carver guessed a blizzard was coming. He was right, and it kept him holed up for the rest of that day and all the next. He was snug enough, sheltered among a clutter of giant rocks at the foot of a precipitous bluff, but several times in the night he woke and listened to the howling of the wind, and hoped that yet another rock would not choose that particular night to come crashing down on him.

After the storm the snow was deep and soft and powdery, and Carver was forced to work harder than the dogs,

134

running ahead of the team and stamping out a trail with his snowshoes. Yet he was glad the blizzard had come when it did, for ahead lay a wide flat plain, in summer a mosquito-ridden swamp, but now frozen as hard as the river. Had he been caught out in this open land by the weather his hardship would have been severe indeed. Instead he was able to travel in reasonable comfort, as on either side the hills receded away until they were dwarfed by distance, and the river divided into a myriad wandering ribbon-like channels.

It took him two days to cross the flats, and then the hills converged again, towering steeply above the river on either side, their flanks black and shaggy with dense stands of spruce and lodgepole pine. Here the ice was roughened and jagged, thrown up into tortuous peaks and valleys, so that at times Carver was forced to manhandle the sledge through a slippery frozen maze where one slip could prove fatal. A wrenched ankle or twisted knee could leave him helpless, trapped among the ice floes until he froze to death. So Carver moved carefully, not daring to relax until the river widened and the ice levelled out somewhat. Looking back, he pondered on the condition of the river in summer, and guessed that if it was difficult to negotiate when frozen, it would be impassable in the warmer months, when white water foamed and thundered through the gorge.

He was now eight days out on the trail, and during that time he guessed he had travelled more than two hundred miles. He must by now be getting close to his goal, but so far he had seen no sign of habitation, nor, except for the ubiquitous ravens, any form of life at all. Still, the weather held fine, and the going was easy.

Now the river wound through attractive park land, with tall trees growing amid rounded snow-covered hills. The river was wider now, and Carver guessed it was also deep. There were no rocks protruding above the ice, and none of the raised gravel bars that told of the wild turbulence upstream. Each succeeding bend and curve lured him on, each fresh vista delighting his eye after the monotony of the wide flats.

The squalor of the settlement, when he came upon it, was in stark contrast to the beauty of its surroundings. It stood on a low bluff overlooking the river, a litter of tumbledown shacks and ragged, decaying tents. The snow-covered shore was stained and mired, strewn with the remnants of rotting hides, broken sleds and the crumbling remains of canoes amid a tangle of yellowing bones, skulls and antlers. Over all hung a yellow shroud, a miasma of smoke and condensation, that smelled as evil as it looked, a blend of dog, wood smoke, rotten meat and ordure.

Carver's immediate reaction was to give the place as wide a berth as possible. He had no wish to become involved with a band of half-starved Indians. He was about to turn his team and make a detour across country when he saw the boat, a wooden stern-wheeler anchored just upstream of the village and frozen fast in the ice. It could only belong to the fur trader he sought, and since a wisp of smoke curled lazily from a chimney on the forecastle, it appeared that he was at home.

Carver whipped up the dogs and headed towards the boat, stopping by the shore and staking the team out in the snow. Then warning Handsome to stay on guard, he slung his rifle over his shoulder and stepped out on to the ice. Further downstream a pack of dogs yapped noisily from the bank, and a small knot of Indians stood silently by, watching him with the apathetic stare that was the hallmark of the defeated. Carver reached the gangplank and was about to set foot on it when a voice hailed him from above.

'I'd take it kindly if you'd hand up that there rifle before you come aboard.'

Carver looked up and found himself gazing into the twin barrels of a shotgun. Holding it was a small brown pixie of a man with a face like a withered apple. He wore a yachting cap to which he had stitched an enormous pair of fur ear flaps, which sat either side of his head like a pair of small rodents. He grinned happily at Carver as he spoke, and Carver smiled back, but he noticed that the hands that held the shotgun were very steady. With a shrug he eased the rifle off his shoulder. The man had nothing to gain by shooting him, and he wasn't likely to be going anywhere for a while. Besides, he still had the Colts. He took the rifle by the muzzle and offered it butt first.

A delighted cackle greeted the gesture. 'A gentleman, I see. Come aboard, stranger, but mind the wires.'

Carver climbed the gangplank to find the deck crisscrossed with wires, strung at varying heights. Tied to these were an assortment of cans, tin plates, mugs and spoons, any one of which falling on deck would make a clatter which would be immediately heard by anyone below. More deadly was a single wire attached to the door of the fo'c'sle, for the ends were tied to the triggers of sawn-off shotguns, bolted to stanchions, and angled so that anyone opening the door would be blasted from both sides by a blanket of shot.

Carver eyed it warily. 'Anyone ever fall for that?' he queried.

Another cackle greeted his ear. 'One did. Looked like a bad case of smallpox for a week.'

Carver nodded. 'I'll believe.'

He turned to get a better look at the boat's owner. The rest of the man was in keeping with his hat. He wore two shirts, one of thick woollen tartan, and over that one of fringed buckskin, black with grease and age. His legs were clothed in caribou-skin pants, and on his left foot he wore a moccasin. His right leg was missing, and in its place was

137

a stump of curiously twisted ivory. It was some moments before Carver recognized it as a sawn-off length of narwhal tusk.

Its owner bowed from the waist. 'Welcome aboard. Name's Stirk, Captain Noah Stirk, out of Whitehaven, Cumberland, England, late whaler, fur sealer, and now agent for the Northwest Trading Company. What's your name?'

Carver told him. 'I have some pelts to sell.'

Noah beamed. 'I pay the best prices on the river. You won't get a better deal this side of Seattle. We pay in pure gold.'

Carver considered this. 'What's the value of gold these days?'

Captain Stirk glanced round him, as though the boat were suddenly crowded with eavesdroppers. 'Twenty dollars an ounce,' he whispered conspiratorially. 'And that's a better deal than you get most anywhere else. Furthermore, if you spend your gold in my store, I buy it back at twenty-two dollars to the ounce.'

Carver looked at him pityingly. Last he'd heard, gold was worth little more than seventeen dollars. So he guessed he would be selling his pelts cheap, and then paying high prices for goods in return. 'And I'll bet your beans are just the cheapest in the territory,' he murmured. 'You don't mean people still fall for that that old con trick?'

Captain Stirk grinned sheepishly. 'Not often nowadays. Still, it's always worth a try. I'll tell you what I'll do. I like the cut of your jib, so we'll trade at an even eighteen dollars, buying or selling. You won't . . .'

'I know,' said Carver. 'I won't get a better deal this side of Seattle. You got whisky?'

'Whisky I got, beans I got, bacon, flour, sugar, lard, biscuits, canned goods. Tea, coffee, tobacco, matches, blankets, woollen stockings, corset stays, bangles, beads, mirrors, axes . . .' His voice trailed away from lack of breath. 'No candles. The Siwashes chew them like gum.'

Suddenly Carver made up his mind. 'I got fresh moose meat on the sledge. You care to put some coffee on the boil, I'll go and hack us off a couple of steaks. When we've eaten, then we can talk about trade.'

Captain Stirk cheered up considerably. 'I'd appreciate some fresh meat. How do you fancy some bacon and beans?'

Carver grinned. 'I thought you'd never ask.'

The smell of bacon frying greeted him when he got back to the ship, making his mouth water and his stomach contract.

Captain Stirk was in the cabin, busy over the stove, his back towards Carver. 'Take a seat,' he called. 'And while you're about it, take off your parka and unship those cannon you're wearing round your waist.'

Ruefully Carver did as he was told. 'How d'you guess they were there?' he asked.

Stirk laughed. 'I could see the bulges. It was either guns, or else you had a double hernia.' He set a mountain of bacon and beans in front of Carver and rummaged round for a fork. 'Mind, you'd never have had time to use them.'

Carver thought of the shotgun levelled at his chest, and felt thankful he had not tried. 'You manage this outfit on your own?' he queried.

The little man nodded, his mouth full of moose steak. 'Just me and the cat.' He waved his fork in the direction of the bunk, and with a start Carver realized that what he had taken for a bundle of pelts was a full-grown lynx, regarding him with a cold amber stare.

Carver shuddered. 'Best to keep that one well fed,' he remarked.

'Why not? She pays her way, keeps the ship free of vermin and scares the hell out of the Siwashes. They

139

call her "the devil cat". Actually she's just a big softie. Raised her from a kitt, and she's never even scratched me.'

'They bother you much?' asked Carver.

'The Siwashes? Good as gold mostly. Course, they're a light-fingered lot, but then that's their nature. Never did have any sense of property. No, it's the white men that try my patience.'

'White men?' echoed Carver. 'There can't be all that many. I haven't seen more than two in a year, and one of them was dead. Anyway, I thought they were all digging for gold on the beach at Nome.'

'Nome's finished,' said Stirk. 'The gold's worked out. Most of the miners have gone back home. There's a lot of them though still up in the hills, working the small creeks all year long. They're no bother. It's the others that cause the trouble. Wanted men mostly. They can't go home, and they can't cross over into Canada because the Mounties are waiting for them, so they roam the river in gangs, robbing and stealing from Indian and white man alike.' He paused, pointing his knife at Carver. 'You want to watch out. Wear those Colts where you can reach them in a hurry. There's one gang in particular. Leader calls himself a fur trader, and sure, he always has plenty of furs for sale. But he never buys no goods for barter, and he never sets no traplines. So how does he get his furs? You answer me that.'

Carver pondered the question while he shovelled beans into his mouth. 'Maybe he pays for them with gold. Maybe he mines gold,' he ventured.

Stirk gave a short bark of derision. 'Him, dig for gold? I've seen his hands. They're as soft as a ten-dollar whore's.'

Carver promised to keep a wary eye open for fur traders with soft hands. 'Surely we're too far north to be troubled by that sort of character,' he remarked. 'I should have thought they'd all be down the Yukon.'

'Yukon's getting too civilized for them these days,' mumbled Stirk, busy with his knife and fork.

Carver doubted that, but let it pass. After they had eaten the captain produced a bottle of passable rye, and Carver had little to do but drink and listen, for Noah enjoyed a good yarn. By the end of the evening Carver had learned all about a long and eventful life.

It was a long time before he could get to sleep that night. He had declined an invitation to spend the night in the stuffy little cabin, and with whisky fumes swirling in his brain he had made his way back to his sledge. Now he lay wrapped in his sleeping robes, gazing up at the stars while Handsome snored softly at his back. The northern lights were at play, sending great curtains and folds of greenish shimmering light flickering across the sky. The fact that Captain Stirk found it worth his while to trade so far north, and that he would be here again next year, was reassuring, but at the same time it was a portent, that others would soon be following in his stead. It was more important than ever that they should get the herd north and begin trading as soon as possible.

He spent the next morning trading his pelts for gold and buying all the food and equipment he needed. The little man was scrupulously fair in his dealings, and to his surprise, when the final settlement was agreed Carver found himself in possession of a substantial quantity of gold.

He visited the Indian settlement one day, but did not linger. The natives were an idle, shiftless lot, depending on supplies from Captain Stirk, which they obtained by trading furs. The women were dirty and louse-ridden, the men surly and suspicious of his questions. There seemed to be little of the customary joy and laughter among the tents. Carver could not help but compare their lot with that of the Nunamiut. Though the nomads too were filthy

141

and verminous, and their habits sometimes disgusting, at least they had a dignity and zest for life he could not help but admire. For these people there seemed no future, and no hope.

Carver wondered what would happen when the thaw came and the captain sailed away downriver after the break-up of the ice. He knew that, contrary to popular belief, spring rather than winter was the time of starvation in the north, and he guessed that for miles surrounding the camp the land was just about denuded of both firewood and game. The people would just have to move on, he supposed, but many of them would die before they found fresh hunting grounds.

The following day he hitched up his team, adjusted his snow goggles and bade a final farewell to Captain Stirk. Then he headed off back upriver. The little man stood on the prow of the boat and watched him disappear into the rising sun, until the glare of the ice hurt his eyes. Then he turned, and went back into the gloom of the fo'c'sle. He had, he knew, been over-generous in his dealings with the stranger, but then, he had enjoyed his company. Better still, he had enjoyed buying his furs. He had come late in life to his strange love, but it was nonetheless strong for all that. He was, he told himself, an extremely fortunate old man.

On the second night of the trip back Handsome appeared unduly restless, and Carver knew why. It was the time of the year when the wolves were running, and Carver guessed there was an unmated female somewhere nearby. So he kept a close eye on him, but despite his vigilance the dog managed to slip away.

Carver cursed. He could only hope that Handsome would return by morning. Meantime he would have to do without his hot-water bottle for the night. He was also without a guard, and remembering Captain Stirk's warning he kept the two Colts fastened to his belt, outside his parka where he could reach them in a hurry.

The night was very still and dark, and stars twinkled in the velvet bowl of the sky, their light reflected in the snow. There was no sound save the occasional whimper from one of the sled dogs as it stirred in its sleep, and the crackle and hiss of the logs on the fire. Carver drew the moose robe tighter round his shoulders and huddled close to the fire, but even so his back was cold.

Three men watched him from a thicket across the river. 'What do you think?' whispered one.

'I dunno,' replied another. 'He's got a rifle. And see those Colts? He could lay down a whole curtain of lead if he got touchy. Looks dangerous to me.'

The third man had also seen the Colts. He was called Lapak, after the island on which his mother had been born. His mother had been an Aleut, a child slave in the house of a rich Russian in Sitka. After Secretary of State William Seward bought Alaska from the Russians for seven million dollars she found herself penniless but free. Since she had discovered at a very early age that men were going to use her anyway, she decided they might as well pay for the privilege, and in the years that followed she learned to her surprise that those who did pay were on the whole much gentler and kinder than those who did not.

Lapak's father must have been one of these paying customers. He grew up, at first the spoiled darling, and later the tout and bodyguard of a large house in Sitka, filled with young ladies who shared his mother's philosophy. He was paid a commission on every client he found, and he supplemented his income by robbing those customers too drunk to recall the events that led up to their loss. He was happy there, for the house supplied his every comfort, and he might never have left Sitka had not an epidemic of diphtheria robbed him of his mother and his life style overnight.

143

He was twenty years old, and there was news of a gold strike somewhere up the Yukon. Where there was gold there would be brothels and drunken miners, and he knew how to manage both. There he met a half-breed named Skinner, so called because of his proficiency with a knife. He was practising his skill on a prostitute when Lapak clubbed him unconscious.

When he came round Lapak gave him an ultimatum: 'Work for me, or hang,' and Skinner, realizing that Lapak could provide him with both pleasure and profit, agreed.

After the Yukon gold rush ended they moved to Nome, where a third member joined the team, a giant of a man called Bull, whose speciality lay in squeezing a man's head between his hands until he lost consciousness. Bull did this so gently that the victim felt no pain, but tended to suffer from memory lapses ever after.

In Nome they prospected for gold, the gold that other miners had dug, in the tents where miners lay asleep, or in lonely cabins along the creeks. Then, when the gold on the beaches finally ran out and the miners departed south, they turned their attention to fur trading.

Lapak provided the respectable front, with his charm and friendliness, and his sledge load of trade goods which never grew less. The others trapped the furs.

Their technique varied. If the victim was alone, Bull held him down while Skinner persuaded him to reveal the whereabouts of his cache. If they came upon an Indian or Inupiat village they usually took one family hostage, and again Skinner was called upon to demonstrate his skill. Normally it was not long before the villagers agreed to part with their furs, and occasionally small quantities of gold. Meantime Skinner enjoyed himself.

The one flaw in this otherwise well-ordered routine was that they could never return to the same place twice. Now they were forced to range further and further afield. They dared not go south, and over the border in Canada the mounted police were waiting for them. So they went north, enduring the hardships and the bitter weather of winter in the hope of one last rich haul.

Now Lapak studied the lone figure sitting in the light of the fire. Gold prospector or fur trader? He could not be sure which, but the man had valuables on his person. Lapak could see the barrels glinting in the flames. He coveted those guns, and they were worth going to a little trouble to acquire.

Very slowly and deliberately he lifted his rifle and took aim. The bullet caught Carver square in the forehead and spun him backwards off the log on which he sat.

Lapak lowered his rifle and squinted at the huddled form lying near the flames. 'Looks pretty harmless now,' he said mildly.

They found the gold, though they were a little disappointed by the amount. Lapak took the Colts, and he was well pleased. They were, after all, the greater prize. They left Carver where he lay, and when Handsome returned the next morning he found the body of his master lying in the snow. Throughout that day and the next he lay beside it, heedless of the clamour of the sled dogs tethered nearby. When night fell the she-wolf began to call, and Handsome stood up. A couple of times he licked Carver's face and whined, but there was no response. After a while he trotted off into the night.

Abner and Ootek waited in vain for Carver's return, and his disappearance was the subject of many a discussion round the fire at night. Several times Ootek suggested he take Anak and ride off in search of him, but Abner would not countenance the idea. There was no way of knowing where he had gone, or how far he had travelled. In any case, it would be easy just to pass him by without knowing it. Besides, even if Ootek found him, there was probably nothing he could do, except bury him, if he were dead.

Indeed, he had probably already been buried deep under the snow, or lay drowned under the ice.

Ootek nodded in agreement, but the knowledge that Carver had probably saved his life still lingered, and he felt indebted towards him.

Abner took a more pragmatic view. 'Carver wasn't looking for you. He was looking for a moose. It was the caribou saved you.' And Ootek had to agree. For himself Abner saw no reason to change his plans following the disappearance of Carver. With the coming of spring he felt a growing urgency to resume their journey, and Ootek too was eager to head on north.

The days were lengthening rapidly now. Sometimes, at midday, when the sun shone or the wind blew warm from the south, the musical sound of running water was heard deep under the snow. The upper layer grew soft and sticky, and at night it froze again, coating the land with a hard, glazed surface that broke underfoot, and gashed the legs of man and beast alike. The cries of wild geese echoed overhead as the flocks flew north to their ancestral breeding grounds, and the bald eagle returned, though the river was still bonded by ice.

Now they parted from the river and headed into the hills. Without compass or map to guide him, without even the position of the sun to aid him on an overcast day, Abner always knew exactly in which direction to travel. Though he hadn't the vaguest idea where he was, nor how far distant his ultimate goal lay, he knew, every moment of his waking life, whether he faced to the north or the south, or any other point in between. This was not due to instinct alone, though inherited knowledge may have played its part. Rather it was a continued awareness of his immediate surroundings, a thousand tiny details noted and committed to memory. So, when he stood with his face to the setting sun and the wind blew cool on his right cheek, he knew its direction was from the north-east. The next day, even though there was no sun and no wind, he knew that the ridges in the snow, whipped up by the wind, pointed towards the south west. Thus without conscious thought, he kept the record up to date.

The cows were now heavy with calf, and though the winter was far from spent, the deer knew that summer would soon be upon them. Then life in the lowlands would be unbearable under the heat of the sun. With the slobbery ground underfoot, and the insects to plague them, their calves would not survive more than a few days of life. They sought the hills, and the cooling breeze.

It was Ootek who sighted the wolf. The first glimpse was no more than a flicker of yellowish white, a hint of movement across a distant snow field. For a long while after he looked for a second sight, but to no avail. He decided it must have been a sheep, one of the big solitary rams they saw from time to time, and dismissed the matter from his mind.

Then he saw it again, clearly this time, its bushy tail streaming behind as it loped across a patch of ground denuded of snow. Wolves generally hunted in packs, but he looked in vain for others of its kind. It was closer now, and next time Ootek saw it the wolf was sitting on a slab of stone some distance ahead of the herd, watching them approach.

None too soon Ootek drew Abner's attention to the wolf, and the Chukchi got his Remington from out of its moose-hide case. He had hardly ever fired the gun since he had acquired it, preferring to leave the hunting to Carver, who was much the better shot. Now he lay in the snow and, conscious of Ootek's critical eye, took careful aim. They both saw the bullet strike the rock just below where the wolf sat, sending splinters of stone flying through the air.

The wolf did not flinch, though it did glance idly in their direction when the sound of the shot reached its ears. Abner raised the sights a notch, took a deep breath

147

and gently squeezed the trigger. This time the shot must have gone over the wolf's head, for they did not see it strike. Abner cursed and fed a third bullet into the breech. He levelled the rifle again, but to his astonishment, when he looked through the sights the wolf had gone. The rock was bare, and of its occupant no trace was to be seen.

Neither he nor Ootek had seen it go, though both were sure they had not taken their eyes off it for a moment. Abner shrugged and put the gun away. Only then did he notice the young Eskimo's visible distress. Ootek's face was pale under his parka hood, his whole body trembling.

'That was no wolf,' he muttered. 'Not a wolf, but Carver. Carver's dead, and his spirit has come to torment us for not going to his aid.'

'That *was* just a wolf, Ootek,' Abner said gently. 'A big old wolf that is wise enough to keep out of range. If he comes any nearer I'll get him, and then you'll see.' He spoke with an assurance he did not entirely feel. As a young man he had learned the ways of the white man well, and he had read the bible from cover to cover. Yet he knew that Jehovah was just the white man's name for the Great Spirit in which he already believed, and since the minister had been at pains to assure him that the devil appeared in many guises, this merely served to confirm what he already knew, that the world was full of spirits, some good, some evil. He had asked the minister once, 'If you hadn't come, to teach me about your god, would I have gone to hell?' The minister had said, 'No.' So Abner had asked, 'Then why did you bother?' and the minister had looked sad, and left him alone for many days.

They journeyed on in silence, but now Abner kept the rifle slung across his shoulder, and his eyes constantly scanned the distant hills. Of the big wolf, however, there was no further sign.

It was still there though, and when night came it lay among a clutter of fallen rock, not fifty yards from the herd.

They were high in the hills now, beyond the Arctic Circle and above the treeline, so they only had fuel for a small fire, enough to cook their evening meal. They turned in early, and since the night was calm and there was no cloud they did not bother with a shelter, but lay watching the stars until sleep came. Patiently the wolf lay waiting, watching the dying glow of the fire.

He was, as Abner surmised, an old wolf. Late in the fall his mate had died, and soon after a younger wolf had challenged him for leadership of the pack. The old wolf had defended his right, but without a mate his heart was not in the fight and he had allowed himself to be driven away without serious injury. Since then he had wandered alone, and he had fared badly, an eater of carrion and dung, and scraps that the ravens had left. Now he had to kill again, or die. As the moon rose and the deer cast black shadows over the surface of the snow, he crept forward, inch by careful inch.

One cow had drifted slightly away from the herd, and it was this animal the wolf had singled out as his prey. As the musk of her scent drifted across the snow, borne on the light breath of the wind, saliva flooded the wolf's jaws in anticipation of his strike. One step, two, and the time had come.

The first the cow knew of the danger was when she felt a terrible blow on the side of her neck. Too late she attempted to turn and flee, but by that time the wolf had seized her by the throat. With a strangled bellow of pain she fell to her knees, then struggled to her feet and began swinging her head, desperately trying to jerk herself free.

Grimly, eyes closed, teeth firmly clenched, the wolf held on, even though he felt himself swung through the air and pounded against the snow. Flailing hooves battered his sides and ribs, but his fangs tore through hair and hide and flesh. He felt hot blood begin to flow, heard the bubbling whistle of breath from the torn windpipe, and sensed his victim weaken as she sank to the snow. Then dimly, through the dying gasps of the cow and the pounding of her flailing heart, he heard the thunder of hoof beats across the snow.

Anak hit him squarely in the ribs, knocking the breath from his body, tearing his hold from the cow and sending him skidding across the snow. Abner and Ootek, roused by the uproar, sat up in time to see the big bull rear on his hind legs and stamp down hard. Then they could only watch as he lowered his head to the snow and ploughed forward once more.

In cutting off his antlers and leaving him with two short stumps Abner had probably equipped Anak with a better set of fighting weapons than nature had invented. Now he scooped the wolf up between two curving prongs and flung him high into the air. As he fell Anak caught him again, and though by now the wolf was quite dead Anak continued to worry and maul the corpse, stamping it into the snow in mindless fury.

At long last his temper cooled, and after a few final desultory kicks Anak left the wolf and returned to the herd. Only then did Abner and Ootek dare approach the kill. They stood for a long time looking down at it in the moonlight.

'A big old wolf, like I told you,' said Abner at length. 'And he's just cost us a cow.'

12

The Hunters

Anak did not escape entirely unscathed from his encounter with the wolf, and when Ootek woke in the morning he was horrified at the sight that greeted him. Anak stood a little apart from the herd, his head slightly to one side, and the hair of his face and neck matted with dried blood. When he had attempted to gore the stricken wolf one antler, in ploughing through the snow, had struck a rock with such force as to dislodge it from its socket. In attempting to free himself from the irritation, Anak had shaken his head repeatedly through the night, and as a result the stump hung down, attached by no more than a shred of skin.

Under no circumstances would Anak allow Abner near him, so Ootek had the task of severing the remaining portion of hide with his hunting knife. At the pain of the incision Anak bolted, but he only ran a few yards before turning, holding his head on one side and regarding Ootek with a mildly inquiring air. Then he trotted back and began to lick the stump Ootek held in his hand, with every sign of relish.

There was little risk of infection while the weather remained cold, and mercifully no flies to lay their eggs in the wound, but there was a danger of frostbite. Ootek left him licking the stump while he collected dry sphagnum moss, which he larded with bear grease. When he had covered the wound he laid a dried rabbit pelt over the pad of moss and tied it in place with strips of rawhide. Then he cleaned away the dried blood with handfuls of snow. The broken stump of antler he kept, but the wolf pelt was not worth saving.

The weather was overcast and dull, with high cloud threatening snow that never came. Each day they climbed ever higher into the hills. Each crest, when they reached it, revealed yet more mountains stretching away into the distance, their peaks white against the leaden sky, the whole landscape a monochrome of black and white and grey. As they steadily gained height, so the temperature fell. The mountains seemed to breed their own weather, drawing currents of icy wind up from the valleys, wind which tore at their clothing and rippled the coats of the deer before sweeping on to rip clouds of frozen snow from the peaks.

The constant threat of a blizzard howling down from the north and destroying them with its fury made them anxious to cross the range, to be free of this forbidding landscape and safe in the shelter of the valleys they were sure must lay beyond. Even the deer seemed disinclined to linger, and though the herders kept up a steady pace throughout most of the day there were times when, after they had made camp for the night, they could look back and see the site they had left that morning.

The temperature never rose above freezing, and at night it fell even more. Without fuel they could make no fire, and they had to eat their meat raw. This was no hardship to either man, in fact they often preferred to eat it uncooked. Fresh raw liver, seasoned with a little of the gall, was a special treat for them. They sorely missed the means of making a hot drink however, and they were forced to quench their thirst with melted snow from the water containers they carried beneath their robes.

Each night they made a temporary shelter in the snow. Where it was deep enough they dug a *miliq*, which was a rectangular pit with a raised sleeping bench on either side, and a roof of skins weighted down with rocks or snow. Where the snow cover was sparse they built a *killigun*, with raised snow-block walls over which to stretch their

152

skins. Though the temperature inside seldom rose above freezing, these shelters were warmer than tents without fire nearby to heat them.

The reindeer were impervious to the cold. Their long thick coats were made up of countless hollow hairs, ultra light yet forming an insulating layer which kept their skins near blood heat, though the temperature might plummet to sixty degrees below zero. Even their muzzles were protected by soft silky hair. It was the skin of the reindeer, and their wild cousins the caribou which, made into clothing, enabled a people to survive the rigours of the most hostile climate in the world.

The threatened blizzard did not arrive, and at last the day came when the travellers stood on the mountain divide, and instead of seeing the endless peaks rising in serried array before them, they looked down on billowing hills stretching away to misty plains. The deer surged forward now, trotting in their eagerness to find fresh pasture, and Abner and Ootek were left trailing behind. They finally caught up with the herd when it stopped to graze in a sheltered valley, and the men rested as the animals pawed away the snow and tore at the rich moss underneath.

The going was easier downhill, and the snow covering thinner, but the deer set such a pace that the two men had to work hard to keep up with them. Even then, they sometimes lagged far behind. Towards the end of the second day, when Ootek caught up with Anak he climbed on the bull's back and rode until they stopped for the night. It crossed his mind that Abner might resent him riding, but he need not have worried. When Abner caught up with them he was grinning broadly.

'You do good to ride,' he observed. 'Keep up with the herd. Prevent attack from wolves.'

So it came about that Ootek was the first to sight the hunters. They were waiting among the rocks at the neck

153

of a narrow valley, watching the herd as it wound its way down the slope of the hill. It was clear that they had mistaken the reindeer for a herd of wild caribou, and had noticed Ootek at the very last moment.

Now they emerged from their hiding places among the rocks. There were seven of them altogether, dressed poorly in caribou skins, and in their hands they held short bows armed with stone-tipped arrows. The leading reindeer had halted at the sight of them and now milled irresolutely among the scattered rocks, bunching together as the rest of the herd caught up with them.

The expressions on the faces of the hunters were blank, impassive, as each man strove to grapple with the emotions that surged through him. What they had thought to be a wild caribou herd turned out to be under the control of one man, one who could work powerful magic, for how else could anyone charm a wild *tuktu* bull into carrying him wherever he wished? Disappointment and dismay at being deprived of their kill gave way to astonishment and a profound respect, for who knew what such a mighty *shaman* could do?

On seeing there was no immediate danger to the reindeer herd, Ootek dismounted and hurried forward to meet them. At his approach the men drew back a pace or two, but after a moment one of their number laid down his bow, and stepping forward greeted Ootek by taking both his forearms and shaking them. He was a little man, his legs slightly bowed, and his back bent with the weight of his age. A dark wisp of beard clothed his chin beneath a drooping black moustache, and what few teeth he had left in his mouth were broken and discoloured. He looked utterly weary, his whole bearing that of a man defeated and crushed, and his breath when he spoke smelled of carrion. Yet his eyes were like those of a falcon, fearless and keen.

In an accent so thick Ootek could barely understand his speech, the old man made him welcome. His name, he said, was Takumik, and he and his brothers were hunting caribou. They were three days' journey away from their families, and if they did not kill soon they would have to return, while they still had the strength to do so. Winter had been hard, Takumik said. 'Many empty sleeps' was how he put it, and some people, the old and the very young, had died as a result of starvation. Hearing this, Ootek recognized the smell of the man, and it reminded him forcibly of the time his own people had died, many of them not from starvation, as they supposed, but poisoned from eating meat that was in an advanced state of decay.

By this time Abner had joined them, and Ootek drew him a little to one side. They still had a quantity of moose meat, and the remains of the bear. In addition they had saved the meat from the dead cow, and had eaten little of it except the liver and heart. Earlier Abner had grumbled about the pack animals being overloaded. Now Ootek urged him to give the remainder of the deer to the men.

At first Abner demurred. 'They'll want more,' he muttered. 'One carcase will not go far among so many.'

'If they want more,' Ootek pointed out, 'they'll try to take it, and even if we kill them all we'll probably lose a few cows in the process. They'll shoot them before we can stop them. Anyway, that's beside the point. These people are starving, yet they've offered us no violence. The least we can do is to give them meat, if only to enable them to stay out on the hunt a few days longer.'

Reluctantly Abner agreed. 'Tell them they can have meat,' he said. 'But choose your words carefully. Try and do it so they think we are just being hospitable. Don't offend the old man.'

Ootek hurried back to the group. 'Takumik must be a great hunter,' he began, 'to have survived so long in the land of his people. Yet it is well known that even the best hunters have bad luck from time to time, even though the fault is not their own. We recognize this, and

155

hope you will do us the honour of accepting meat for you and your men, for you will hunt even better on full bellies.'

He waved his arm to the two hide bundles Abner had laid in the snow. 'It is little enough,' he went on, 'and poor stuff compared with what you are used to, but we hope it will help.'

The effect of this speech on the old man was dramatic. He seemed to grow taller, to stand straighter, and he turned to the others, speaking so rapidly that Ootek could not understand him. Immediately everyone grew more cheerful, and one or two licked their lips. Some, who had been looking surly at the sight of so many deer they were not allowed to kill, broke into smiles, but no one made a move towards the bundles.

Takumik turned back to Ootek. 'We thank you,' he said simply. 'No doubt we will kill soon, and there will be laughter in the tents of our people once more. Meantime, it is good to share meat with friends.'

At a sign from Takumik two of the men picked up the bundles of meat. Then the hunters drew away to one side, watching as the reindeer herd moved on down the valley. They were still standing there when Ootek looked back some time later, tiny specks in the emptiness of space.

Two nights later they reached the flat lands at the foot of the mountains. In summer the region was virtually impassable, a maze of lakes and ponds and muskeg swamps, interspersed by sluggish streams meandering aimlessly across the quaking land. Where the ground was drier dense stands of spruce and poplar grew, so close together that those which had died, or been uprooted by the wind, had no room to fall. So they leaned at all angles, one supporting the other, forming a tangle it was impossible to penetrate without cutting a way through.

156

Now the slobbery ground was frozen hard, offering a firm crossing, but the trees made it impossible to plan a straight route. As darkness fell, and they sat enjoying the luxury of the first fire for many nights, they debated whether to try to find their way through the trees or to keep to the higher ground at the base of the hills. Neither man knew how far the swamp lands extended, but they realized there was a danger that the herd could become fragmented and scattered, with individual deer falling prey to wolves. Better, perhaps, to take the longer, safer way round.

Hardly had they reached this decision when they heard a soft cough, somewhere out in the darkness. Abner reached for his rifle and both men jumped up, stepping out of the firelight into the safety of the shadow, listening and waiting until their eyes became accustomed to the darkness. To their surprise it was Takumik, with a younger man he introduced as Putu, his son.

'We bring you caribou tongues,' he announced. 'Next day, after you left us, we kill many deer. Two men now journey to our village to get help bringing in the kill. Others stay to guard the meat. We come to thank you, and to warn you not to go any further. Turn back, if you do not wish to die.'

Ootek and Abner looked at him in dismay. 'We must go on,' said Abner. 'Our way lies north, and we have come too far to turn back now. What dangers lie ahead?'

'An Indian village. Bad people. Kill Inupiat, rob them of their meat, steal their children and wives. We fear they will rob you too, if they see your deer.'

'How many Indians?' asked Abner.

For answer Takumik held up his hand, fingers and thumb splayed wide, and opened and closed it four times. Then he gazed at it perplexedly for a moment and shook his head. 'And many more,' he said.

Ootek explained their plan for skirting round the flat lands, but once again Takumik shook his head. 'The

Indian village stands on a hill,' he explained. 'From there they can see all around.' He hesitated a moment, and then went on, 'There is a way, through the mountains over towards the rising of the summer sun. It is hard, and the mountains are steep, but there is a way through, a narrow gorge where the sun never shines. If you wish, we show you.'

Abner looked thoughtful. 'This gorge. I don't like the sound of it. We could be walking into a trap.' It occurred to him that Takumik could have planned the whole thing from the start, and concocted a yarn about hostile Indians to win his trust. Perhaps the other hunters were not guarding meat at all, but waiting somewhere along this ravine for Takumik to lead them in. Then he remembered the caribou tongues. They must already have killed many deer to get them. Perhaps they had, but perhaps they were allied to these Indians, and were helping them to get meat too.

He shook his head. It all boiled down to whether they could trust Takumik or not.

As if he had spoken out loud the old man echoed the thoughts that had been racing through Abner's mind. 'You ask yourself whether you should trust this Takumik or not. How can you be sure he is not leading you into some sort of trap? So I tell you that I will lead you into the gorge, and if the Indians should come upon us then you will see me kill at least one of them before I die. If I do not, then you may kill me yourself.'

'Why?' asked Ootek. 'Why should you do this for us?'

The old man stared for a long time into the fire, and when he looked up his face was that of a young warrior, confident and proud. 'They say that most men hunt to live, but my people live to hunt. I have made many great kills. I have met the great white bear, alone, and slain him with my spear. For this and many other feats I hope my people will remember me. Now perhaps I grow too old to

158

hunt, and yesterday's kill might be my last. Now I wish to leave my people one last memory of me. If I can no longer hunt, I would like to choose the place, the time, and the manner of my death.'

He laughed like a young boy. 'Not every man may be so fortunate. So, you see, I am not doing this for you, but for myself, and if I get a chance to kill some of those river vermin at the same time, then I shall die with a song on my lips.'

He laughed again. 'But maybe the rest of you do not want to die just yet. So I will try to guide you safely through this land.'

Before they slept that night they roasted some of the caribou tongues, and while they were waiting for them to cook Takumik told them the story of how he killed the polar bear, taunting the great beast until it reared on its hind legs and charged, only to impale itself on Takumik's spear. 'I should have died that day,' chuckled Takumik. 'But I lived to tell the tale. Maybe I shall live to tell many more.'

Abner grinned in the firelight. 'I do not think you want to die just yet, old man. Maybe you should take a young wife, and tell your stories to her.'

Takumik shouted with mirth. 'Then I would die quickly,' he replied.

That night Ootek was a long time falling asleep, and when he woke, long before dawn, he found he was sweating freely under his robes. At first he thought it was just the unaccustomed heat from the fire, but when he threw off his robes and stood up he could feel the wind warm upon his face. He knew it was no more than the false promise of spring, and that at any time the weather could grow bitterly cold once more, but if the snow started to melt it would make the going difficult for both deer and men alike. Still, there was nothing he could do about it, so he went back to his bed and fell asleep once more.

159

The morning dawned grey and overcast. The warm south wind still blew, bringing with it large wet flakes of driving snow. To add to their misery the snow surface was soft and sticky, balling up under the thongs of their snowshoes and making them heavier with each step. The unaccustomed warmth affected the deer, making them sluggish and slow to move, so that tempers were generally frayed before the whole herd was on the move.

Only Takumik seemed unperturbed, and almost danced with glee at the sight of the snow, pointing out that it would reduce visibility and so make their passage safer. 'No filthy Indian move in this weather,' he chuckled.

In this he was wrong. At the very moment he spoke two young men of the tribe, one pulling an empty sledge, were setting off into the foothills. The day before one of them had killed a moose and cached the meat. Now they were anxious to retrieve their harvest before it was buried by the snow.

Takumik had warned the others that the going was hard, and they very soon discovered he had not lied. The trail wound through a series of low, hummocky hills, their flanks sloping so steeply that at times even the deer found it difficult to get a grip on the soft slippery snow. Rather than tackle the slope direct they chose to weave their way upwards, twisting and winding, treading wherever the terrain gave the surest foothold. Behind them the men slithered and cursed, the swirling snow stinging their eyes and clinging to their clothing. Progress was slow, even when they were moving downhill. Only Takumik seemed to be able to move freely. He flitted ahead, wraithlike, appearing and disappearing in the snow.

Then, quite suddenly, the weather changed. The wind dropped, the snow ceased to fall and the clouds gave way to clear skies and brilliant sunshine. Before them stretched a landscape of ice-cold blue and purest white. High above, the mountain peaks were stained rose pink and gold, and the dark rocks stood etched in black against the snow.

All saw now that they stood at the summit of a pass high in the hills. Ahead of them stretched a broad valley, narrowing in the distance, while on either side the mountain slopes grew progressively steeper, until they terminated in sheer walls of rock. It was at that moment that Ootek, gazing round and marvelling at the grandeur of the scenery, distinctly glimpsed a human form on the skyline opposite.

He called out to Takumik, who was higher up the slope, pointing in the direction he had last seen the figure, and Takumik, shading his eyes against the sun, confirmed that not one, but two men had stood there watching. Now, though, they had vanished.

Abner was inclined to dismiss the incident, but Takumik was clearly worried. 'We must go fast, fast, before they bring others.'

'But it's too far for them to come,' protested Abner. 'They'll never get back to the village and fetch the others in time to catch us.'

Takumik shook his head violently. 'Not too far,' he protested. 'Look! I show you.' Swiftly he drew a sketch map in the snow at their feet. His people had been drawing such maps for centuries. They had a strong awareness of their location in time and space, and an encyclopedic knowledge of their hunting grounds. Takumik was no exception, and looking at his map Abner and Ootek knew it to be accurate.

It showed the camp they had left, and their tortuous trail through the mountains. Now Ootek saw that they had been drawing nearer to the village all morning. They were now almost level with it, and but a short distance away. It would be easy for the Indians to cross the hills and lie in ambush for them.

'We must turn back,' he ventured.

161

It was Putu, the silent one, who answered him. 'They will expect us to do that, and send a party to our rear to wait for us.'

They had no choice but to press on, Takumik leading, with Abner by his side, his Remington resting in the crook of his left arm. Putu took the right flank, climbing high on to the slope of the hill, the better to be able to see across the valley. Ootek brought up the rear, his shotgun at the ready.

Now the sun had passed its zenith and was hidden behind the mountains to the west. Ahead one side of the valley lay in deep shadow, and already it seemed that Abner and Takumik had vanished into a hole in the earth, the deer following them, dissolving like smoke in the gloom. Once they were out of the sun the temperature plummeted, and Ootek shivered in the chill, pulling his robes about his shoulders. On either side the slopes of the mountains stretched up sheer, their flanks bulging ominously with snow. The air was very still in the gorge, and the sounds of the herd, the grunting and lowing and crackling of hooves, came echoing back as if from the bottom of a pit.

Putu left the slope and came to join him, glancing back over his shoulder from time to time.

'How far now?' asked Ootek.

'Long way yet,' said Putu. 'Still much danger. Maybe they wait for us further down the valley.'

They hurried on. Despite the cold, Ootek found he was sweating, the gun slippery in his grasp, and his snowshoes weighed heavy on his feet. Ahead the gorge widened out a little and the slopes of the mountains were less steep. Away to the left a fold in the hills gave way to another gorge, similar to the one they had just passed through and walled in by sides so steep that the peaks seemed to lean inwards, as if to threaten anyone who dared to pass through.

To his dismay Ootek realized that the deer in front of him were no longer moving forward but milling round in confusion. Dead ground hid Abner and Takumik from view, and anxious to discover what was causing the delay Ootek pushed forward, leaving Putu to guard the rear.

At first he was certain that Takumik had led them into a trap. The valley ended in a sheer drop, its sides encased in ice, where in summer a waterfall cascaded over the cliff. There was no way down as far as he could see. Then he noticed a narrow ledge that wound, first upward, then down the slope of the mountain to the flat plain. Abner and Takumik were vainly trying to persuade the leading cows to take the first steps along the ledge, but this they steadfastly refused to do.

Ootek took a few steps along the ledge. The surface was of hard rock, slippery with ice, but it was quite wide. An overhang forced him to duck his head slightly, but it was not so low as to hamper the passage of the deer. At no point did it appear particularly steep or treacherous, and Ootek was sure that if only one deer could be persuaded to venture on to the ledge the rest would follow.

He made his way back into the centre of the herd and caught Anak by his one remaining antler. Without haste he led the bull forward, past the cows and out on to the ledge. At first Anak baulked, blowing wildly down his nostrils as his feet felt the surface of the ice. Talking to him all the while, Ootek tugged gently, urging him forward, step by careful step. Once he was firmly on the ledge Anak moved forward with growing confidence, and one by one the cows began to follow. Now Anak could not turn back, even had he so wished, and Ootek abandoned him, leaving him to find his own way down. Then, his back pressed tight against the mountain wall, Ootek watched the herd file slowly by.

A sudden shout alerted him. Something was wrong back in the valley. Slowly, so as not to panic the deer into slipping over the cliff, he began to edge his own way back along the ledge.

Men were running towards them, not down the valley they had just travelled but down the canyon to the side, tiny figures silhouetted against the snow. Even at that distance Ootek could see they were armed, some with spears, some with bows to which arrows were already strung.

There was no mistaking their intention. Clearly they had hoped to reach the herd while it was still confined to the valley, and they had almost succeeded. Half the herd still waited to join the others on the ledge. There was no hope of saving them. In a very short space of time they would be slaughtered under a hail of arrows, or stampeded over the cliff edge. At that moment it dawned on Ootek that he too was probably going to die. Almost before the leading runner was within range he grabbed his shotgun and fired.

The shot whistled harmlessly over the heads of the pursuers, but in the confines of the gorge the detonation sounded like a thunderclap, rolling and echoing round the hills and causing the runners to come to a sudden stop. The reverberations died away. Then, in the silence that followed there came a sullen distant roar, a dull series of explosions that grew and mingled until they became one unbroken cataract of sound.

Far away on the hill the runners paused, and as one man they turned and began to run back the way they had come. High above them the mountainside seemed to dissolve in smoke as the pregnant slopes released their heavy overburden of snow and the whole mass, laden with moisture, came cascading down. Great boulders, torn from their beds in the rock, rained down to land with earth-shaking force on the steep mountainsides, releasing yet more snow. In an instant the whole scene was obliterated in a grey blanket of fog.

164

It took a long while for the snow cloud to clear, but when the last shreds finally dispersed, the hill looked utterly devoid of life. Of the enemy no trace was to be seen. Ootek never knew whether they had escaped or if their bodies lay buried deep under the snow.

Abner surveyed the devastation in silent awe. 'That was quite a shot,' he said at length.

Ootek looked inordinately pleased with himself. 'For the first time,' he announced, 'I remember to fire only one barrel.'

With the last of the reindeer moved on to the ledge, Takumik and Putu took their leave.

'We are in your debt,' said Abner.

Takumik laughed. 'No. It is I who owe you, for you have given me yet another tale to tell, about the gun that brings down mountains when it speaks.'

Together father and son watched the reindeer herders descend to the safety of the flat land. They were still standing there when Ootek turned and saluted them one last time. Then he hurried after the deer, already strung out along the trail. When next he looked back, the men had gone.

Still the sea coast seemed no nearer. Ahead lay a broad, rolling expanse of tundra, and beyond that in the far distance more mountains, their peaks veiled with smoking wraiths of cloud. An ice-laden wind whistled and moaned across the barren land, piling the snow in billowing dunes and waves, and whipping up clouds of fine granular snow that blinded them and stung their cheekbones. Even the deer seemed reluctant to face the weather and slowed their pace to a crawl, until it became obvious that they would not gain the shelter of the mountains before darkness fell.

Without fuel, or shelter of any kind, the two men spent a miserable night. Sleep eluded them, despite the fact that both were exhausted after the rigours of the day, and long

165

before first light they were ready to move on. The deer lay scattered across the tundra. Each had sought out what little shelter it could find, settling in the lee of the snow drifts, and during the night snow had piled up against them, making them all but invisible in the gloom. One by one grey shadows materialized out of the ground, moaning and protesting as they shook themselves free of snow.

Morning dawned clear, and for a while the wind dropped, making travel easier. Already, though, mares' tails were forming high in the sky, foretelling more wind to come, and ominous dark clouds began to mass along the southern horizon. Yet the mountains of the north to which they journeyed seemed as far away as ever. They could do nothing but hurry on, for both knew that a great storm was coming, and to be caught on the open tundra meant certain death.

Looking back Ootek saw that the clouds had grown darker, more menacing, filling the sky with great billowing mushrooms of vapour. Jagged forks of lightning flickered and played around the edges of the clouds, and already they could hear the distant rumble of thunder.

The first blast of the wind hit them like a slap from a mighty hand, forcing them to their knees and driving the breath from their bodies. Grimly they struggled to their feet and fought their way on. Like a veil the first fall of snow swept towards them, whirling dark flakes swirling and driving, shutting out the light of the sun. Ahead, the deer panicked and ran before the storm, leaving the men alone in the vast emptiness of the tundra.

They could only cling together, each supporting the other and fearful lest they should be separated in the gloom. Mercifully the storm was at their backs, otherwise progress would have been impossible. Even so, it seemed that they had been spared from slaughter by the Indians only to suffer a similar fate at the hands of nature. The lightning flashed more frequently now, and the thunder rolled and crashed above the howling of the wind. All the while the temperature fell lower and lower, numbing their minds and driving all sensation from their limbs.

Then suddenly Ootek felt the ground give way beneath him, and beside him he heard Abner wail in anguish, certain he was falling to his death. Next moment they had landed on soft snow. All around them the reindeer were huddled for protection, and the wind howled harmlessly overhead.

The river had saved them. Over the centuries it had ground its way across the barren land. Each spring the snows had melted and the bonds of ice had broken, and the waters had flowed to the sea, bearing with them a burden of silt and rock, digging down ever deeper into the frozen land. Now the bank on either side stood taller than two men, and it was down one of these banks that Abner and Ootek had tumbled.

They barely had strength to find their sleeping robes. Together they huddled down at the base of the cliff, their arms around each other, sharing their body warmth. There they fell asleep, while the storm raged harmlessly overhead.

13

The Summer of Friendship

All that day the storm raged, and with the coming of night the wind increased in intensity. Towards dawn it began to weaken and die, and an eerie silence spread over the land. When Abner and Ootek woke they were stiff and cold, ravenous with hunger and parched with thirst, but they were alive, and sleep had given them renewed energy.

It took them a little while to discover a way up the steep side of the river, but at last they found themselves on the open tundra once more. At first the going was easy. The mountains looked closer now, and the wind had packed the snow down hard. Gradually however the flat terrain gave way to a nightmare jumble of small hills and rocky outcrops, a series of pitfalls and traps in which the drifted snow lay deep. The deer struggled and floundered, constantly wandering into blind alleys and having to turn back, or sinking shoulder deep into soft snow. Dusk was falling once more before they reached a sheltered valley in the hills, with dwarf willow for fuel and shelter, and browse for the hungry deer.

They remained there resting for the next few days, until after a while the deer grew restless and they were forced to move on. The days grew longer. The sun climbed ever higher into the sky, and although the temperature barely rose above freezing, the absence of any wind made the weather seem almost springlike.

The fine weather held and they made good progress, covering twelve, fifteen, sometimes twenty miles in a day. Yet always the land stretched interminably before them, and there were times when both men despaired of ever reaching their goal. Low hills ascended to jagged mountain peaks, narrow valleys widened into desolate open tundra, frozen lakes, muskeg swamps and wooded flats intersected by winding rivers.

The brief Arctic spring advanced north behind them, its arrival heralded by the passing of birds, flocks of wild geese and swans, sandhill cranes and lesser ducks and waders. The wind, when it blew warm from the south, melted and dried the snow drifts, eroding them into fantastic shapes. In the primrose-yellow light the twigs of the stunted birch trees glowed wine red, and eagles soared once more in the skies.

The reindeer cows were heavy with calf, their sides bulging, their body muscles wasted and shrunken with the rigours of the long journey and the scarcity of good browse. Yet still they journeyed on, until late one afternoon they topped a rise in the hills, and there, far out on the horizon, shining silver and gold in the sinking sun, lay the sea.

At last it seemed to both Abner and Ootek that the end of their quest was near. Here, surely, Ootek would meet others of his kind, and somewhere near lay the valley Abner had journeyed so far to find. They stood for some time surveying the scene. It was impossible to tell, from this distance, where the land ended and the sea began, for sea ice still stretched out far beyond the actual shore. Beyond lay open stretches of water, but even that was littered with drifting floes. The land between them and the shore consisted of rolling treeless hills, their sides in shadow, their snow-clad crowns stained pink by the sun. To the north the white ribbon of a river curved south to the sea, and beyond that high cliffs faded into the misty distance. At the river's mouth a long arm of land jutted like a bear's paw out towards the sea, and in its protection lay a scattering of small huts.

They made camp that evening in a sheltered valley some distance away from the village. The rolling land hid the settlement from view, and they felt it prudent not to reveal the existence of the herd until they knew what manner of people inhabited the place. Meantime there was an abundance of dwarf willow, the dry twigs of which gave them fuel for their fire, and plenty of rich grazing for the deer.

Over their evening meal they debated the wisdom of approaching the village. It would be a simple matter to detour round it, or alternatively turn south and head further down the coast. Yet both men, though reluctant to admit it, were hungry for human companionship.

Ootek pronounced himself willing to go alone and meet the people. 'The worst they can do is drive me away.'

Abner was not so sure. 'Better by far that both of us should go. One man alone cannot guard his rear.' So they agreed to risk leaving the deer unguarded while they made the short journey to the village.

The settlement consisted of five dwellings, situated close to the shoreline and set into the side of a steep hill that sheltered them from the north and west. The huts themselves were rude affairs, dug partly into the ground, their low stone walls roofed with driftwood and thatched with turf, but they looked solid and substantial.

Only three out of the five turned out to be occupied. In one an old couple cared for their only grandchild. In another lived a young man, his wife and their newborn baby. The third was occupied by an older couple, their son and two teenage daughters. Long before Abner and Ootek reached the settlement the barking of sled dogs staked out in the snow warned the people of their approach, and by the time they were within hailing distance the entire population was assembled on the beach, awaiting their arrival. The men all held spears, even the old grandfather, but they did not look particularly belligerent. Abner and Ootek had both brought their guns but they were careful to keep them slung across their backs, and they kept their hands in view at all times.

Abner had taken the precaution of bringing along the last of their moose meat, together with a liberal portion of fat, and this more than anything helped to allay the suspicions of the people. A fire of driftwood was quickly kindled on the shore, and as the meat roasted they talked. The older man, whose name was Kavik, told them that times had been hard but were now better, and improving all the while. On this stretch of the coast the whales stayed far out to sea, and so the whalers did not come. It had been many years since they had seen a white man.

'They brought us guns, like you carry, but without the black powder that makes them fire they are less use than clubs.'

Kavik told them they were able to hunt seal and walrus, and in the summer they caught salmon from the river, snared birds and collected their eggs. Once they had hunted caribou, but two summers ago non came.

'Last year a few. This year perhaps many. Now though we are hungry for meat that does not taste of the sea.'

Looking at the ring of expectant faces, their eyes fixed on the sizzling meat, Abner could see that this was so.

The meat was barely done, but they could wait no longer. Abner and Ootek were careful to take only the smallest of portions, but even so the meat did not go far among so many. When all had vanished Kavik spoke in a low voice to his wife, and immediately she and the younger woman got up, to return with dark steaks of seal meat, small white cubes of blubber, and seal oil in a bowl carved from driftwood. Now it was Ootek's turn to look hungry, and as he and Abner dipped pieces of blubber in the oil and savoured the sweet-sour taste he felt a glow of warmth and happiness such as he had not experienced in a long while.

The oil was strong, and it made them both cough. This caused a great deal of merriment, and the grandfather looked at them knowingly.

'You have been a long time away from the sea,' he remarked.

Abner nodded. Kavik's reference to the whalers had aroused his interest. A large whaling fleet would provide a good outlet for reindeer meat. They would also trade for ivory and furs. It occurred to him too that Kavik might have some knowledge of the valley he sought.

He would have like to confer with Ootek before he revealed the existence of the reindeer herd. Yet now was the time to explain their quest if he wished to discover what he needed to know. As simply and as plainly as he could he related their story. He ended by explaining that since the cows were shortly due to drop their calves, they wished to remain in the neighbourhood for a while, until the young deer were strong enough to resume their journey.

There was a long pause after he had spoken, the men indrawn and thoughtful, the women whispering among themselves.

Then Igruk, the grandfather, spoke again. 'I have heard of the country of which you speak. It is true that game is plentiful there, and the natives are many and wealthy. Already they trade with the whaling crews, but their village lies far, far away to the north. Still, I can tell you how to find it if you wish to journey so far.'

'Meantime, you wish to trade with us?' queried Kavik.

Abner nodded. 'We need new outfits, clothing and boots such as your women can make, and as you have noticed, we have a longing for a taste of the sea. In return we can offer our surplus meat. Moreover, we can help with the hunting, and the butchering of walrus and seal.'

Later in the day everyone in the village, even old Igruk and his wife, accompanied Abner and Ootek back to the valley where they had left the herd. There they marvelled at the sight of the deer, seemingly unafraid of man. 'Like so many big dogs,' was how Kavik described them. When they departed they took with them the dismembered

172

carcase of one of the gelded caribou bulls.

Next evening they held a feast, with everyone, includ-ing Abner and Ootek, crammed into the largest of the dwellings. First, there was Eskimo ice cream. This was made from whitefish, boiled and flaked and whipped up with melted reindeer fat, and flavoured with crushed blueberries. Everyone had to sit very quiet and still while it was being made, for the people believed that any noise made the mixture too heavy.

Meantime the reindeer ribs were roasting and the tongue and liver simmered in a pot. The head had been made into soup, and there was salmon, smoked and dried, and fish eggs, and small seabirds pickled in seal oil. There was sourdock and wild chives mixed with oil, and *masru*, the Eskimo potato.

The long hours of daylight ended and twilight fell, but still the feast went on, until every last scrap of the reindeer had been consumed. Then old Igruk got out his drum, and one by one the people began to dance.

As the temperature rose so they shed their clothing, their bodies shining with grease and sweat as they swayed in the smoky light of the oil lamps. Urged on by the remorseless rhythm of the drum Ootek and Abner scrambled to their feet and joined in the dance, writhing and twisting until the heat, the smoke of the lamps and the smell of sweat and body odours made the faces blur and the walls spin, and they collapsed exhausted on the floor.

Two days later they were fitted with their new clothes, *ugruruliks* – boots made from the skin of the bearded seal, the hair turned inside – together with light seal-skin parkas and pants, with undershirts of fawn skin. Later, they were promised, they would have a full set of winter clothing each.

So began the summer of friendship, when Ootek resumed his education as one of the Inupiat, or 'real people'. Kavik, and the younger man Kuvlu, taught him to handle a kayak,

173

and showed him how to harpoon the ringed seals that hauled out on the ice floes. Though he killed the occasional seal, he never attained the skill of the other men.

When the ice went out of the river and the salmon ran upstream to spawn, Abner and Ootek helped the people to build dams, trapping the great silver fish on their journey and spearing them as they lashed the water to foam. They climbed the cliffs to the north in search of eggs and young seabirds, and netted the adults as they flew close to the cliffs. When the wild geese were moulting and unable to fly they clubbed them as they ran cackling over the tundra.

Best of all, Abner and Ootek enjoyed the excitement and danger of the walrus hunt. These great beasts came north in the spring, and the people hunted them on shore, where they hauled out to bask in the sun, or on the ice floes out to sea, paddling out in their big *umiak* and harpooning them when they lay on the ice. Because of their great size, for some of them weighed over a ton, and particularly because of their uncertain temperament, the people considered them very dangerous prey indeed. An angry walrus could sink a boat with his tusks, cutting the skin hull to shreds, or one might try to climb aboard, sinking the frail craft with its weight.

On the first hunt Abner took his rifle and succeeded in killing a walrus with a single shot as it lay on the beach. The next time, however, they were in the boat, and the pitching and tossing of the waves made it difficult to aim. He fired seven shots before he killed, only to see the walrus sink to the bottom of the sea. After this the people told him to leave his gun behind.

Because of the danger, the people took the hunting very seriously indeed. Before the hunt Igruk stripped to the waist and made an invocation to the little creatures that lived at the bottom of the sea, asking for calm water for the hunt. No joking was allowed, and under no circumstances

174

was anyone permitted to speak disrespectfully of the quarry.

When Kavik sank the heavy harpoon deep in the body of the walrus the water was lashed to foam, and the *umiak* was towed at frightening speed as the victim, secured by a stout seal-skin line, tried to escape. While Kavik and Kuvlu stood by with their spears, Abner and Ootek manned the paddles striving to keep the *umiak* from capsizing. After the kill came the long voyage home, towing the great carcase behind them. Then, after the butchering there was feasting and dancing, and the surplus meat was buried underground where the permafrost would preserve it. (Next winter it would be used as food for the dogs.)

Meantime the reindeer herd prospered. The calving was particularly successful, the herd almost doubling in size. No wolf or bear came near to menace the calves, and as summer advanced they moved the herd down on to the coast near the village, away from the heat and flies. The adults grew sleek and fat. Anak now sported a new set of antlers, which spread and arched in a great sweeping curve over his head, and showed no sign of any deformity from his injury. No wild caribou came near the coast that year, but Abner gave the people one of the gelding bulls from time to time, and they were content.

As the summer ripened, Ootek began to take an increasing interest in Kavik's two daughters. The elder, Oluu, was the more beautiful, tall and slender, with a gentle serious manner. Pavek, the younger, was smaller and chubbier, always joking, or laughing at someone else's wit. Both were hard workers, expert at dressing skins and never without a piece of sewing in their hands.

Ootek could not make up his mind which of the two he preferred. One day he would be certain it was Oluu, the next he favoured Pavek. Both girls seemed equally attracted to him, and neither appeared to bear any resentment when he paid undue attention to the other.

175

Indeed it was impossible for him to be alone with either one for more than a short while before the other appeared, as if by accident. Sometimes one would just happen to be passing by, or the other would approach with some innocent query, to interrupt an intimate moment. It was not long before Ootek began to suspect they did it on purpose.

Oluu had a pair of hip-length seal-skin boots, snow white and close fitting, fringed at the top with polar bear. The long hairs bounced seductively as she walked, and the first time Ootek saw her wearing them the vision was so tantalizing that his mouth went dry, he stammered, and began to blush at the audacity of his thoughts. Pavek thought this hilariously funny, and ran to join her sister, mincing along beside her and swinging her fat little bottom in comic pantomime. Oluu was unperturbed, and seeing the effect the boots had on Ootek, wore them at every opportunity.

For his part Ootek showed off just as shamelessly, riding Anak along the beach to win the admiration of both girls, and wrestling the bull to his knees, an old trick in which Anak was the compliant accomplice. He brought them presents, necklaces made from sea shells or reindeer teeth, bracelets of mink tails, fur ties and mitts, a set of toggles he had carved from the stump of Anak's antler, which he had carried with him all this time.

He grew heedless of the passage of time, so it came as a profound shock when one evening Abner announced that it was time for them to move on once more. Ootek sat stunned. He had been so happy for the past few months that he had forgotten Abner's ambition to trade reindeer meat for furs and gold and walrus ivory. He did not share Abner's dream of material wealth. Right here he had found all the riches he desired. Furthermore he had not the slightest wish to trade with the white whalers. They had brought him enough misery in the past.

Not for the first time he found himself at a crossroads in his life. Alone that night, he pondered the problem. Materially, he lacked nothing he wanted. They had long since run out of the few trappings of civilization they had acquired. Neither he nor Abner possessed tobacco or matches. To make fire they used Abner's file, which when struck with a flint produced a shower of sparks. Without the file Ootek could make fire with a bow and drill. It took a little longer, that was all. He had his shotgun, and a supply of cartridges still, but he could well live without them. Their tea was exhausted, and their sugar and salt, but he had no real need of such things.

He did have a need for Oluu, or Pavek. He still could not make up his mind which girl he preferred. He loved them both equally, and it had occurred to him that as a wealthy reindeer herder he could afford to take them both as brides. He was sure Kavik would not mind. Yet he did not think they would leave the village that was their home to follow him into the unknown, and he feared to ask, lest they refused him.

He *could* abandon Abner and the deer, and become one with the people. Yet he knew that without the reindeer his status would diminish. He would never become a great hunter. After so long an absence from the coast he had forgotten much of what he had learned during his childhood, and sometimes he despaired of ever being able to acquire the specialist skills possessed by these hunters of the sea. He felt he would become a poor relation, a burden on the tribe, a useless wastrel who could not even support one wife, let alone two. So he was forced to admit to himself that, like Abner, he too desired wealth, but of a different kind and for different reasons.

With a pang of regret he thought of Kyloo. She had been crippled and scarred, another misfit like himself, yet she had been tender and caring, and asked for nothing he could not provide. She had been willing to follow the reindeer

177

herd, but had been unable to withstand the rigours of the life.

Then there was Abner to think about. Abner was older than he, but not too old to take a wife. He seemed to have no interest in Oluu or Pavek, but how would he react during the long lonely nights of winter if Ootek had two brides, and he none? Such a situation could only cause trouble.

That night he slept badly, and all next day he was so quiet and withdrawn that in the evening Abner ventured to ask him what was on his mind. They had pitched their tents near the shore, where the wind from the sea protected them from the attacks of the flies, and they were sitting on the pebbly beach, looking out across the grey tumbling waters of the sea. The deer were nowhere to be seen, but Ootek knew they were not far away, hidden by some fold in the land. Suddenly, the solution to all his problems came to him.

Screwing up his courage, he asked, 'One day, when you have many many deer, will you give me a few of my own? With the big bull?'

Abner looked at him in surprise. 'Why? We're partners aren't we? As long as you stay with me, you have equal shares.'

Ootek shook his head in consternation and dismay. 'I don't want equal shares,' he stammered. 'Just a few cows, and the bull.'

Abner studied him for a while, but Ootek offered no further explanation for his request. He did not need to, for Abner had watched the young man closely throughout the summer, and knew quite well what lay in his heart and mind. In a way Abner was glad that Ootek had found the happiness he sought, but found it hard to suppress a pang of regret at the thought of losing him. He had grown fonder of Ootek than he had realized during the time they had spent together.

178

'As soon as there are cows to spare,' he promised, 'you shall have them.'

Ootek hugged his knees in an effort to contain the wild elation that filled him. Not this winter, nor maybe the next, but one day he could return here with his own herd, and marry the beautiful daughters of Kavik. Now he was content to wait. He told no one of his plans, and fortunately it did not occur to him that in the intervening time Oluu and Pavek might find other suitors, nor that one year the wild caribou might return and the people would not need him, nor his reindeer.

The wild geese were flying south. In the mornings new ice crackled on the margins of the lakes. Berries were picked, seal oil stored in skins, dried fish cached, meat stored deep underground where the permafrost kept it fresh. Driftwood was stacked high near the houses and the boats stowed away. The people were ready for the winter. Abner and Ootek were fitted with new clothes, made from the reindeer skins they had supplied. As a parting gift they gave the people the last of the gelding bulls, and on a bright morning in autumn, when the tundra glowed red and russet and gold in the dying sun, the herd moved north.

14

The Stranger

So far Lapak and his team had failed to find the riches they desired. Settlements were few and far between and the villagers poor, if they were not actually starving. Days, sometimes weeks passed without them finding another living soul. Both Skinner and Bull were growing more surly and discontented with every day that went by, and Lapak realized that soon their partnership was to be dissolved. He intended to leave with a whole skin and a good percentage of the profit.

In camp at night, after they had eaten and were sitting round their fire before turning in, he pondered ways of severing his relations with the other two. He could simply harness up his sledge and leave, but their haul of furs took up most of the room on all three sledges. It was unlikely that the other two would allow him to load the whole consignment on to his, even if there had been room.

He thought of killing the other two, but then, in order to carry enough food for himself and the dogs on his journey, he would have to cache most of the furs until he could collect them at a later date. That would involve three long and tedious journeys, even supposing he could find the cache again. Regretfully, he realized he was stuck with the others as surely as if he were their prisoner, and he guessed, correctly, that Skinner had come to the same conclusion. Each man was safe from any harm coming to him from the others, at least until they drew nearer civilization. Even then Lapak was confident that the others would do him no injury, for they would be relying on him to negotiate the sale of the pelts.

The worst of the winter was almost on them. Soon rapid travel would be impossible. They wanted one last goodly haul of furs, and then they could turn back. The difficulty lay in where to find it. One of their problems was not being able to speak more than a few words of the native language, so they were unable to question their victims closely as to the whereabouts of other settlements. Without a map or guide they had only the haziest notion of their whereabouts.

It was also inadvisable to return by the route they had travelled. There and then Lapak came to a decision. In the morning they would turn west and head for the sea, following the coastline back south. There would be settlements by the coast, and furs and walrus ivory. The others greeted the news with enthusiasm. They too had had enough of the wilderness, and longed for the freedom and comfort of civilization.

Two days later, as they topped a rise in the hills, Skinner, who was in the lead, threw out his snow hook and stopped his team. When the others reached him he was dragging his rifle from its case on the sledge.

'Caribou,' he grunted, pointing down the slope.

Lapak gazed down at the snow-covered valley. 'There's someone else hunting them,' he observed quietly.

Skinner looked closer. On the far side of the herd he could just make out a small, skin-clad figure walking slowly towards the deer. Yet he carried no gun, nor any other weapon as far as he could see. What was more curious was that the caribou did not seem in any way alarmed, but just carried on pawing away the snow and grazing as if the proximity of man posed no threat whatsoever.

Suddenly Lapak let out a low whistle of surprise. 'They're reindeer,' he exclaimed.

'Reindeer?' queried Skinner.

'Sure, and that man is their herdsman. I remember hearing about reindeer being shipped here from Siberia.

Nearly twenty years ago it must have been. They raise them for the meat. Last I heard they were making around a hundred dollars apiece. How many deer do you reckon there are down there?'

Skinner did a rapid count. 'Over two hundred, bulls, cows and calves. Two hundred times a hundred? Why that's twenty thousand dollars on the hoof down there, if we could get them to market.'

'Since we were planning on heading that way, why don't we take them along with us?' said Lapak thoughtfully.

Skinner was all in favour of driving his dog team down into the valley and taking over the deer herd straight away, but Lapak advised caution. 'We don't know how many more men there are down there beside that one. Nor how well armed they are. We don't want a shooting war.'

After some discussion it was agreed that Lapak should drive his sledge down there alone, while the others waited back in the hills. Once there, Lapak would make some excuse to worm his way into the man's confidence, find out how many companions he had, and decide what to do from there.

'If there's only him, or one other, it will be easy,' he said. 'I'll stay the night, and when they are asleep two quick thrusts with a knife will do the trick. If there's more than two, I'll make my excuses and leave, and we'll try and find some other way round the problem.'

Before Lapak set out he unloaded his sledge of all food, but he kept the pelts to give the impression he was an honest fur trapper. He also kept the two Colts he had recently acquired. As he was about to leave, a final thought came to him.

'If you hear a shot,' he said, 'come on down. It means the deer are ours.'

Abner and Ootek watched the sledge draw near. As it approached they saw that something was amiss with the

182

man who followed behind. He seemed to sway and stumble as he ran, and as it came to a halt he lay forward across the handles, coughing so that he was unable to speak, and waving aside their queries in feeble protest.

They led him to their fireside, and Abner heated soup for him to drink while Ootek staked out his dogs. Then they waited for him to recover, curious to hear his story. Wolves, he explained, had stolen his meat cache over a week before, and since then he had been unable to find any food, for himself or his dogs. He'd thought he had found himself a caribou herd, but now he saw the deer belonged to them, he was wondering if they could sell him some meat. He could pay, with gold if they wished.

They fed him then, with thick stew containing large chunks of meat, and he bolted it hungrily, as he imagined a man who had been a week without food might do. Between mouthfuls, he expressed his gratitude.

'Sure don't know what would have happened to me if I hadn't met you good people. . . Times like these a man needs a friend on the trail. . .'

Ootek, watching him, thought: He's too fat. He's too damn fat to have gone a week without food. A man's starving, his eyes go sunken and his cheeks hollow. His are round and fat. Man eats like that, first time for a week, he'll throw it all back up in the snow. He's keeping it down.

He looked at Abner, but the Siberian seemed totally unsuspecting. Ootek turned to study the dogs in the snow. They had curled up and gone to sleep, though the smell of the meat from the fire must have been strong in their nostrils. Ootek grew more and more uneasy, though he could not for the life of him tell why. He continued to watch the stranger, and noticed that although he appeared to be engrossed in his food, his eyes were darting everywhere around the camp, as though he were assessing them and their belongings. From time to time he glanced back up at the hills whence he had come, as if he were watching and waiting for someone to appear.

Finally Lapak put aside his plate and sat back, belching loudly. 'Boy! That was good!' he exclaimed. 'You folks manage this herd alone then?'

Abner nodded. 'Just me and Ootek here.' He looked across at Ootek, but the young Eskimo was gazing vacantly into space, seeming to take no notice of the stranger or his conversation.

Lapak slapped his knees with his hands. 'Well, I guess if you folks will excuse me, I'll wrap myself in my robes and sleep off that meal awhile. Sure is nice not to feel hungry for once.'

He had not asked them to feed his dogs, Ootek noticed, nor shown any concern for them. He continued to watch the distant hills, for what he wasn't sure. For a long time nothing moved or stirred, and then he saw it. It was just for a fleeting second, and then only once, but in that moment Ootek knew he had seen the smoke from a fire, a faint wisp that curled up over the horizon and then was gone. Now he was certain someone waited up there, and he knew that somehow they were connected with the stranger in his own camp.

He said nothing to Abner about his suspicions. For one thing, he was sure that the older man would merely scoff at his fears. For another, he couldn't be sure that the stranger really was asleep. He lay unnaturally still. Most people, in Ootek's experience, did not sleep like that. They tossed and turned, flung their arms about, and snored. This one didn't even breathe like a man asleep.

Darkness fell and Abner and Ootek ate their evening meal, but the stranger did not stir. Ootek continued to watch the hills, hoping to see a light or the glow of a fire, which he could show to Abner as evidence of his fears, but there was nothing, only the stars and the soft reflected light of the snow. Before he turned in for the night he slipped a cartridge into each barrel of his shotgun and softly closed the breech. When he lay down he did so on his left side, the fingers of his right hand curled around the stock of the gun, the barrel cradled in the crook of his left arm and resting alongside his cheek. If anyone came near to threaten him, he only had to move the muzzle a few inches to aim and fire.

He had taken the precaution of making sure that Abner lay between him and the stranger. It was a little unfair of him, he thought, to put Abner in the line of first attack, but he reasoned that if *he* remained alert and watchful Abner would come to little harm. He lay still and gazed at the stars, watching the slow progress of the Great Bear as it scribed a wide circle round the pole star.

Despite his fears, his eyelids grew heavy. The stars began to swim, and soft waves of sleep came lapping at the shores of his waking mind, when suddenly the stranger sat up. Ootek came wide awake. He gripped the gun and waited as the man scrambled out of his robes and on to his feet. Then, to Ootek's mingled surprise and relief, he walked a short distance away from the camp. Next moment Ootek heard him urinating in the snow.

Without a word or even a glance in his direction the stranger returned to his robes and curled up as if settling to sleep once more. Almost, then, Ootek relaxed, convinced now of the man's innocence. He chided himself for his stupidity, calling himself an old woman for nursing such groundless fears, and prepared to surrender himself to sleep. Then suddenly he knew. With a certainty that jolted him wide awake, he realized that this had merely been a test. If one of them had woken and challenged the stranger at that moment, the man would merely have apologized and no suspicions would have been roused. As it was, the man had used the call of nature to check that they were

185

both asleep. The attack, if it was to happen, would come soon.

The fire, which had burned down low, suddenly flared into life. For a brief moment the flames flickered and glowed, lighting the bodies of the recumbent men. Then the blazed died, but a small flame lingered, burning with a steady clear light, casting a rose-pink glow over the snow. With a slow stealth that was totally alien from his movements a short while ago, the stranger crept from his robes. Watching him, Ootek caught the gleam of a naked knife. Very slowly, he slid the muzzle of the shotgun free of his robes.

Bent double, and moving with infinite care, the man crept across the short expanse of snow that separated him from Abner. When he reached his side he stopped. Ootek's finger tightened on the trigger of his gun. Then he hesitated, watching in the tiny light of the flame, for instead of attacking his victim the man had paused for a moment as if in thought, and then begun to tiptoe round the sleeping form of Abner, until he had his back to Ootek.

Then Ootek saw why. Abner lay on his left side, the breadth of his right shoulder protecting the vital area around his heart, where the stranger would need to strike to ensure a swift kill. Sure enough, the stranger laid a hand on Abner's shoulder and began to roll him over on to his back. With the speed of a striking lynx, Ootek slid from his bed. When the muzzle of the shotgun was no more than a hand's breadth away from the back of the stranger's head, he took a deep breath and fired.

15

King of the Wild

Abner was having a dream, in which he rode Anak, down a narrow gorge over which hung snowbound cliffs poised precipitously above his head. Ootek was pointing his gun, and Abner was begging him not to fire.

There was a loud bang, and he woke to fresh nightmare. Someone had his hand on his shoulder, and as he rolled on to his back he saw Lapak's face looming over him, suffused with the ruddy glow of the fire. As he stared, uncomprehending, Lapak's face seemed to explode, disintegrating like an overripe pumpkin, and Abner was spattered with bits of skin and blood and tiny sharp splinters of bone, which blinded him so he could not see. There was a great weight on his chest and he was unable to breathe. Only the frantic pounding of his heart told him he was still alive, though convinced he was facing his last moment on earth.

Then he heard Ootek, laughing and crying, babbling in his native tongue, and next moment the weight was lifted off him and he was free to breathe again. He sat up, wiping the blood and mucous from his face with his hands, staring in mingled horror and disbelief at the corpse which had pinned him to the ground.

'Wha. . .What happened?' he gasped.

'He had a knife,' said Ootek. 'He was going to kill you. Both of us.' And Abner could see that this was true. The knife lay where it had fallen, glinting in the snow.

Swiftly Ootek told Abner of his earlier suspicions, and how he had lain awake, expecting such an attack. 'There

187

are others,' he added. 'Somewhere up on the hill. I don't know how many, or where.'

'They will have heard the shot,' Abner said. Both men stood, listening and staring out over the hills, but there was nothing to see, no lights, and no movement, and no sound save that made by the last thin trickle of blood flowing from Lapak's shattered head. For a time they stood irresolute, uncertain what to do next. Then Abner slid his rifle from its case and checked to see that the magazine was full. When he looked up Ootek was struggling with Lapak's corpse.

'Help me sit him up,' Ootek gasped.

Abner did as he was told, and together they propped the body in a sitting position by the fire, and Ootek pulled the hood of the parka over what was left of Lapak's head. Then he plumped up the bedding he and Abner had been lying on, so that in the dim light it looked as though they still slept, or had died there. He was not a moment too soon. When he looked up again the virgin expanse of snow upon the shoulder of the hill was marred by two dark shapes. Two men on foot were hastening towards them over the hard-packed snow.

They looked around for some place of concealment. There was nothing except the sledge abandoned by the stranger, and tugging Abner's arm, Ootek led him towards it. It was a mistake. The dogs, which had lain quiet until now, woke with a chorus of barks and snarls, a bedlam of sound which mingled with the distant thunder of hooves as the deer stampeded away. Appalled by the noise, Abner and Ootek could only lie in the shadow of the sledge and hope that the dogs' traces did not give way.

They knew they could not stay there. After their first outburst the dogs had subsided somewhat, but they kept up an intermittent yapping and grumbling that threatened to betray the men to anyone who drew near. Ootek lay in the snow and considered the problem. The deer had

188

checked their headlong flight, and in the silence he could hear the crackling of their hooves and their low grunting as they began slowly to drift back. They at least would afford some shelter.

But it was no good, he reflected miserably. They dared not run towards the herd, for then the deer would panic and stampede again. If they tried to walk slowly across the intervening snows, they would be clear targets. Even if they gained the shelter of the herd, at the first exchange of shots the deer would bolt once more, leaving them both exposed.

The deer were drifting closer now, but glumly Ootek realized they would not come much nearer, because of their fear of the dogs. Besides, the men were narrowing the gap faster. They appeared to be approaching without caution or fear, and already he could hear one calling to the figure seated by the fire. At any moment their suspicions would be aroused. He gripped the shotgun tighter, and out of the corner of his eye he saw Abner take aim with his rifle. Then, to his consternation, Abner lowered the gun.

'They're not armed,' he whispered.

It was incredible, but true. Ootek strained his eyes through the gloom, but as far as he could see, neither man carried a rifle. Yet that did not mean they were not armed. He was about to point this out to Abner when, to his horror, the tall Siberian stood up.

'Stand where you are,' he commanded. 'Don't come any closer, or I'll shoot.' As the two men stopped in their tracks, he began resolutely to walk towards them.

This is a mistake, thought Ootek, a bad mistake. Why didn't he shoot them when he had the chance? He was almost sobbing with frustration and despair. The deer were much closer now, and acting on blind impulse he slipped away from the shadow of the sledge and walked softly across the snow, praying all the while

189

that the attention of the men would be focused entirely on Abner.

Somehow he managed to gain the shelter of the herd without being noticed, and mingling with the deer he hunted round until he found Anak. Whispering softly to him all the while, he climbed on to the bull's broad back and, drumming with his heels, drove him towards the edge of the herd, closer to the fire. The two men were sitting down now, Abner still covering them with the rifle. He could hear them talking. Softly he slid off Anak's back, but kept in the shelter of the herd.

'Seems downright unneighbourly,' the big man was saying. 'Waving that gun at two innocent strangers.'

'What do you want here?' demanded Abner.

'Want?' queried the other man. 'We want nothing. We heard a shot, and figuring someone was in trouble, we came on down to lend a hand.'

'There's no trouble,' said Abner shortly.

The big man laughed. 'No trouble? Here's a man sitting with his head blown off, as comfy and as peaceable as you please, and you holding a gun on us, and you tell us there's no trouble.' He turned to his companion. 'Makes you wonder, don't it?'

The other man leaned forward confidentially. 'What I'm wondering,' he said in a low voice, 'is while we're sitting here gossiping like, where's your friend? The one who was sleeping in that bed there? Or have you blown his head off too?'

Bewildered by this barrage of questions, Abner seemed to waver. The muzzle of his gun drooped, and at that moment Ootek saw the knife flash. His gun was pointing directly at the man, and without hesitation Ootek pulled the trigger.

There was a hollow metallic click. In his excitement Ootek had forgotten to eject the empty cartridge from the chamber. Immediately he pulled the other trigger and the gun bucked in his hands. He saw the man blown backwards, but the knife was already curving on its way. He saw Abner crumple and fall forward, his body shielding his gun, and as the big man leaped to claim it Ootek rushed forward, swinging the empty shotgun like a club.

It caught Bull on the side of the neck, with a bone-jarring force that would have killed an ordinary man. Bull grunted and sank to his knees, but as Ootek rushed in to deliver a second blow the big man gave a bellow of anguish and rage. Rearing up, he wrested the shotgun from Ootek's grasp, flung it far into the darkness, and advanced on him with outstretched hands. Unarmed, Ootek knew it would be folly to resist. He turned and fled, hoping at least he could escape into the shelter of the dark.

He ran like a hare, twisting and turning in the night, but above the panting of his breath and the beat of his heart in his head he could hear the steady thud of feet in the snow. They were gaining on him now, and it crossed his mind that he would die all the quicker because he could not catch his breath. Then above the pounding of his heart and the beat of the steps he heard a fresh noise, the thunder and crackle of hooves. Next moment there came the sound of an even louder, heavier thud, and a choking scream that tore the silence of the night.

Twice before he had seen Anak savage a corpse, but never had he seen such unabated fury as the bull now displayed. Though the man must have weighed over two hundred pounds Anak lifted him with ease and threw him again and again. Then he proceeded to pound him into the snow with his hooves. Ootek left him to his work. There was nothing he could do to stop him, even if he had wanted to. Struggling to regain his breath, he made his way wearily back to the fire.

The man he had shot was dead. Of that there was no doubt. He lay on his back, his knees drawn up and his hands pressed against the snow, as if he were struggling to rise, but his mouth was open and his eyes stared vacantly at the sky. Abner was conscious, and he looked at Ootek with a wan smile.

'You're getting right handy with that gun of yours,' he whispered.

Ootek looked at him, sitting half raised, his body propped on one elbow, the other hand shielding the haft of the knife that protruded from his chest. Tears of remorse and anger stung Ootek's eyes.

'I was too late,' he said, 'I should. . .'

Abner did not let him finish. 'You were quicker than I was,' he said.

Dawn was breaking tardily over the low hills. Ootek sat in the grey light, watching over his partner and friend. He wanted to pull out the knife, but Abner waved him away.

'It's not uncomfortable as it is,' he murmured. 'I'd rather die without pain.'

A lump rose in Ootek's throat and he swallowed angrily. 'You're not going to die,' he blurted, but he knew in his heart that he lied.

There was little he could do except make Abner comfortable. He built up the fire and wrapped him in robes against the cold, but when he tried to move him on to a more comfortable bed Abner groaned, and begged him to desist.

Ootek dragged away the corpses of two of the men, but Anak still stood guard over the third, and he dared not approach too near. He heated some food, but he had no appetite to eat, and Abner wanted nothing but a little water to moisten his lips. For a while he seemed to sleep, but next time Ootek looked at him his eyes were open, and a faint smile played around his lips.

192

'You keep the deer now, you hear. Look after them. You've fought for them hard enough.' He turned his head slightly and looked out over the herd. 'You've got more than you wanted, as it turns out.'

Ootek turned away so that Abner would not see the tears that blinded his eyes. When he looked back and tried to murmur his thanks, Abner was dead.

He did break down then, and for a while he let the tears flow freely. Then he scrambled to his feet and got to work. He could not let Abner lie where he had died, in the company of villains. Instead he harnessed up the dogs, loaded Abner's body on to the sledge and drove it up the hill. It was impossible to dig a grave in the frozen ground, so he laid Abner to rest Indian fashion, on a platform high in the trees, wrapped in a moose-hide shroud. Then he took the Remington and shot the dogs.

A distant barking alerted him, and he found the camp and the dog teams belonging to the other two men. These he also killed, rather than let them starve. He parked the sledges under the tree where Abner's body lay. The reindeer herder lay far from the land of his fathers, but he would lack for nothing on his journey to the spirit world. Ootek stood for a moment listening to the sound of the wind in the pines. Then he turned and made his way resolutely downhill.

Next morning he broke camp early, and left the valley. Already the leaves had fallen from the aspens, and small birds flocked through the bare branches of the trees. He walked with the sun on his left shoulder and his eyes set on the distant hills. He was going home, and he was richer than he had ever imagined, even in his wildest dreams. He had left behind him another fortune in gold and furs, but he did not mind. He was to suffer one more loss on his journey, but this time it was one that he welcomed with joy.

*

193

He was a week out on his way, and the weather was holding well. Camped high in the mountains, he was sheltered from the wind by a huddle of ancient, weather-worn stones. Before him the deer were spread out, grazing over the treeless, windswept tundra, and he sat hugging his knees, congratulating himself on his good fortune and dreaming about the summer to come.

Anak was far over on the skyline, grazing on the outskirts of the herd, and suddenly Ootek noticed that the bull was standing, head erect, alerted by something Ootek could not see. All at once he left the herd and trotted purposefully away. Then he stopped, looked back, and slowly returned to the herd. At first Ootek thought nothing of it, but when the big bull did it again curiosity brought him to his feet.

Anak stood staring down the valley, his attitude one of eager expectation, and when Ootek looked he saw a low cloud shrouding the snowfields far, far below. It was some time before it dawned on him what it was. Then his eyes adjusted to the light and he saw that what he had thought was a cloud was a forest of antlers, and the smoke of untold breaths. A herd of wild caribou was passing by. For a moment he stood in wonder and awe. It was the first wild herd he had seen since his days with the Nunamiut. Perhaps it could be the last.

The other deer had not heard them, or paid them no heed if they had. Yet Anak had heard the call, and now he was torn between two worlds. Ootek could guess how he felt, for hadn't he stood at the same crossroads himself? He had been offered a choice in life, the alternative between wealth and power and luxury in the white man's world, or a place with his own people, a place where he belonged on earth. Now the caribou was faced with making the same decision.

A great wave of sympathy and understanding swept over him, though mingled with grief at the thought of

194

the parting he knew must come. He walked up to Anak and buried his face in the dense cape of hair that covered the bull's neck.

'You must go,' he whispered, 'and we must part, for our destinies lie along different trails.'

Still Anak stood motionless, though Ootek could feel the great muscles quivering under his skin. It was as if the bull were eager to depart, yet reluctant to leave his companion behind. Almost as if in a dream Ootek climbed once more on to his back, and at once Anak broke into the steady swinging trot Ootek had grown to know so well. Swiftly he raced down the hill to join the others of his kind.

Suddenly Ootek awakened from his trance. Slipping from the bull's back he whacked him hard on the rump.

'Go!' he commanded. 'Go! Or stay. The choice is yours. We are both free.'

As if in obedience to his command, Anak trotted a short way towards the passing herd. Then he turned and came slowly back. Clearly the bull was asking Ootek to go with him and join the wild herd.

'Go!' he shouted again, louder this time. 'You saved my life. I give you yours. . .*Go!*'

Anak turned again and set off once more, slowly, reluctantly, as though he too grieved at the parting, but this time he did not look back. Ootek watched him go, his proud head with its great crown of antlers glowing gold in the evening light, and a thought came into his head. He remembered once Carver telling him about a great man, a chief who ruled over not one small band, but a whole country. A king, Carver said this man was called, and he wore a strange headdress, a crown of solid gold. He, Ootek, would be king of his own domain, but the big caribou was king of the wild.

He could see Anak no longer, but still the caribou herd passed by. He turned and looked at his own small herd. The wild bull had rewarded him handsomely, he thought, and now he had repaid his debt. He felt curiously light of heart as he set off back to the camp. The deer grazed peacefully beneath the darkening sky, and around him the heedless wind whispered softly over the snow.

Epilogue

Ootek returned to the people with his reindeer herd, and in course of time he married Oluu and Pavek. Between them they had many children, and these produced even more offspring, who were sometimes confused over which grandmother was really theirs. But no one seemed to care very much.

The reindeer herd prospered, so that Ootek was able to buy brides for his sons and provide handsome dowries for his daughters. At the wedding feasts they ate meat that did not taste of the sea, and each autumn, when they harvested the deer, they traded hides and meat for fine furs and other luxuries. Ootek steadfastly refused to trade with the white men. From experience he knew that such dealings brought famine in their wake.

From time to time, though, he gave away deer, to form the nucleus of other herds. Some prospered. Some were stolen by Indians or whites. Some were decimated by predators or disease. Yet slowly, down through the twentieth century, the herds grew in number and size, and today the descendants of the original deer still graze by the shores of the Bering Sea.

Anak lived on to sire many calves, and now, after many vicissitudes, the wild caribou herds still make their annual migrations, north in the spring, and south at the end of the short Arctic summer. Across the vast frozen lands on the roof of the world, they symbolize the inexorable power of life itself.

Ootek's descendants go to high school now, and some attain degrees in medicine and law and the arts. Many, the brightest and best, return like Ootek to the land where they belong. They have learned how the whalers came and went, the fur traders and the gold miners, and now they co-exist with those who drill for oil. One day the oil men too will depart. Only the land and the sea will remain, that which has provided the Eskimos with meat and furs and the indomitable will to survive. This land they have held in trust for the past ten thousand years, so successfully that most of it remains as unsullied and unchanged as it was when they first arrived. It is a record of achievement perhaps unique in the world.